Farewell Waltz

Milan Kundera was born in 1929 in Czechoslovakia and since 1975 has been living in France.

Milan Kundera
Farewell Waltz

translated by Aaron Asher

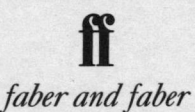

faber and faber

First published in Great Britain 1977 by
John Murray (Publishers) Ltd
50 Albemarle Street, London W1X 4BD
First published in paperback in 1993 as *The Farewell Party*
by Faber and Faber Limited
3 Queen Square London WC1N 3AU
This new translation first published in 1998

Printed in England by Mackays of Chatham plc, Chatham, Kent

There was no Czech edition of this book but there was a French translation
entitled *La Valse Aus Adieux* © Editions Gallimard, 1976

A CIP record for this book
is available from the British Library

ISBN 0–571–19471–0

6 8 10 9 7 5

CONTENTS

First Day

1

Autumn has arrived and the trees are turning yellow, red, brown; the small spa town in its pretty valley seems to be surrounded by flames. Under the colonnades women come and go to lean over the mineral springs. These are women unable to bear children and hoping to gain fertility from the thermal waters.

Men are far fewer among those taking the waters here, though some are to be seen, for beyond their gynecological virtues the waters are apparently good for the heart. Even so, for every male there are nine female patients, and this infuriates the unmarried young nurse who is in charge of the pool used by the women being treated for infertility.

Ruzena was born in the town, and her father and mother still live there. Would she ever escape from this place, from this dreadful multitude of women?

It is Monday, toward the end of her work shift. Only a few more overweight women to wrap in sheets, put to bed, dry the faces of, and smile at.

"Are you going to make that phone call or not?" two of her colleagues keep asking her; one is fortyish and buxom, the other younger and thin.

"Why wouldn't I?" says Ruzena.

"Then do it! Don't be afraid!" the fortyish one responds, leading her behind the changing-room cubicles to where the nurses have their wardrobe, table, and telephone.

"You should call him at home," the thin one remarks wickedly, and all three giggle.

"The theater number is the one I know," says Ruzena when the laughter has subsided.

2

It was an awful conversation. As soon as he heard Ruzena's voice on the phone he was terrified.

Women had always frightened him, even if none of them had ever believed him when he announced this, considering it a flirtatious joke.

"How are you?" he asked.

"Not very well," she replied.

"What's the matter?"

"I have to talk to you," she said pathetically.

It was exactly the pathetic tone he had been anticipating with terror for years.

"What?" he said in a choked voice.

She repeated: "I absolutely have to talk to you."

"What's the matter?"

"Something that affects both of us."

He was unable to speak. After a moment he repeated: "What's the matter?"

"I'm six weeks late."

Trying hard to control himself, he said: "It's probably nothing. That sometimes happens, and it doesn't mean anything."

"No, this time it's definite."

"It's not possible. It's absolutely impossible. Anyway, it can't be my fault."

She was upset. "What do you take me for, if you please!"

He was afraid of offending her because he was suddenly afraid of everything: "No, I'm not trying to insult you, that's stupid, why would I want to insult you, I'm only saying that it couldn't have happened with me, that you've got nothing to worry about, that it's absolutely impossible, physiologically impossible."

"In that case it's no use talking," she said, increasingly upset. "Pardon me for disturbing you."

He worried she might hang up on him. "No, no, not at all. You were quite right to phone me! I'll be glad to help you, that's certain. Everything can certainly be arranged."

"What do you mean, 'arranged'?"

He was flustered. He didn't dare call the thing by its real name: "Well . . . you know . . . arranged."

"I know what you're trying to say, but don't count on it! Forget that idea. I'd never do it, even if I have to ruin my life."

Again he was paralyzed by fear, but this time he

5

timidly took the offensive: "Why did you phone me, if you don't want me to talk? Do you want to discuss it with me, or have you already made up your mind?"

"I want to discuss it with you."

"I'll come to see you."

"When?"

"I'll let you know."

"All right."

"Well, see you soon."

"See you soon."

He hung up and returned to his band in the small auditorium.

"Gentlemen, the rehearsal's over," he said. "I can't do any more right now."

3

When she hung up the receiver she was flushed with anger. The way Klima had taken the news offended her. For that matter, she had been offended for quite a while.

It is two months since they met, one evening when the famous trumpeter was appearing at the spa with his band. After the concert there had been a party to which she had been invited. The trumpeter singled her out and spent the night with her.

Since then he had shown no sign of life. She sent him two postcards with her greetings, to which there was no response. Once, when she was visiting the capital, she phoned him at the theater where, she had learned, he rehearsed with his band. The fellow who answered asked for her name and then told her he would go look for Klima. When he returned a few moments later, he told her the rehearsal was over and the trumpeter had left. She wondered if this was only a way of getting rid of her, and she resented it all the more keenly because she was already afraid she was pregnant.

"He claims it's physiologically impossible! That's marvelous—physiologically impossible! I wonder what he'll say when the little one turns up!"

Her two colleagues fervently agreed with her. When she told them, the morning after in the steam-saturated treatment room, about her indescribable night with the famous man, the trumpeter had immediately become the property of all her colleagues. His phantom accompanied them in the nurses' room, and when his name was mentioned, they giggled up their sleeves as though he were someone they knew intimately. And when they learned that Ruzena was pregnant they were overcome by an odd joy, because now he was physically with them deep inside Ruzena's womb.

The fortyish nurse patted her on the shoulder: "Come, come, dear, calm yourself! I've got something for you." She opened a creased, grubby copy of an illustrated magazine: "Look at this!"

The three of them gazed at a photograph of a young,

pretty brunette standing onstage with a microphone at her lips.

Ruzena tried to make out her destiny in these few square centimeters.

"I didn't know she was so young," she said, filled with apprehension.

"Come on!" said the fortyish nurse, smiling. "This photo is ten years old. They're both the same age. That woman can't begin to match you!"

4

During the phone conversation with Ruzena, Klima recalled that he had been anticipating such terrifying news for a long time. Of course he had no reasonable grounds for thinking he had impregnated Ruzena after that fateful party (on the contrary, he was certain he was being unjustly accused), but he had been anticipating news of this kind for many years now, long before he ever met Ruzena.

He was twenty-one when an infatuated blonde thought of feigning pregnancy in order to force him into marriage. In those harrowing weeks he suffered stomach cramps and finally fell ill. Ever since, he had known that pregnancy was a blow that could strike anywhere at any time, a blow against which there is no lightning rod and that announces itself by a pathetic tone of voice on the telephone (yes, the blonde too had initially given him the disastrous news on the phone). That event of his youth always made him approach women with a feeling of anxiety (though with much zeal), and after each amorous rendezvous he was fearful of disastrous consequences. He reasoned that his pathological cautiousness kept the probability of disaster down to barely a thousandth of one percent, but even that thousandth managed to terrify him.

Once, tempted by a free evening, he phoned a young woman he had not seen for two months. When she recognized his voice she cried out: "My God, it's you! I've been waiting and waiting for you to call! I really needed you to call me!" and she said this so insistently, so pathetically, that the familiar anxiety clutched Klima's heart, and he felt in his whole being that the dreaded moment had now arrived. And because he wanted to confront the truth as quickly as possible, he went on the attack: "Why are you saying that in such a tragic tone of voice?" "Mama died yesterday," the young woman replied, and he was relieved, though he knew that someday he would not escape the misfortune he dreaded.

5

"All right, what's this all about?" said the drummer, and Klima finally returned to his senses. He looked around at the musicians' worried faces and told them what had happened to him. They laid down their instruments and tried to help him with advice.

The first piece of advice was radical: it came from the eighteen-year-old guitarist, who declared that the kind of woman who had just phoned their leader and trumpeter has to be brushed off. "Tell her she can do whatever she wants. The brat isn't yours, it's got nothing to do with you. If she keeps insisting, a blood test will show who the father is."

Klima pointed out that blood tests mostly prove nothing, and therefore the woman's accusation prevails.

The guitarist replied that there wouldn't have to be any blood test. When you fend off a young woman, she's very careful to avoid taking useless steps, and when she realizes that the man she accused is no pushover, she gets rid of the kid at her own expense. "And even if she ends up having it, we'll all go, all of us in the band, and testify in court that we'd all been to bed with her. Let them try to find out which one of us is the father!"

But Klima responded: "I'm sure you'd do that for me. But by then I'd already have gone out of my mind with uncertainty and fear. In this kind of thing I'm the biggest coward, and what I need most of all is certainty."

They all agreed with this. The guitarist's proposal was good in principle, but it was not for everyone. It was especially not advisable for a man with weak nerves. Nor was it recommended for a famous, rich man whom women considered worth the trouble of rushing into a very risky venture. So the band shifted to the opinion that, instead of brushing off the young woman, he should persuade her to have an abortion. But what arguments should he use? They considered three basic possibilities:

The first method was to appeal to the young woman's compassionate heart: Klima would talk to the nurse as to his closest friend; he would confide in her sincerely; he would tell her his wife was seriously ill and would die if she were to learn that her husband had a child by another woman; that both from the moral point of view and because of the state of his nerves, he would be unable to bear such a situation; and he would beg the nurse for mercy.

This method came up against an objection in principle. You could not base an entire strategy on something as dubious, as uncertain, as the nurse's kindliness. Unless she had a really good and compassionate heart, the maneuver would backfire. She would be all the more aggressive because of the insult of the elected father of her child showing such excessive regard for another woman.

A second method was to appeal to the young

woman's good sense: Klima would try to explain to her that he was not and never could be certain the child was really his. He had met the nurse only that one time and knew absolutely nothing about her. He had no idea what other men she was seeing. No, no, he didn't suspect her of deliberately deceiving him, but surely she couldn't insist she wasn't seeing other men! And if she were to insist on this, how could Klima be sure she was telling the truth? And would it make sense to bring into the world a child whose father would always be in doubt about its paternity? Could Klima leave his wife for a child he didn't even know was his? And did Ruzena want a child who would never be allowed to know its father?

This method also proved to be dubious: the bass player (the oldest man in the group) pointed out that it was even more naïve to count on the young woman's good sense than to rely on her compassion. The logic of the argument would be wide of the mark, while the young woman's heart would be shattered by her beloved's refusal to believe her. This would incite her, with tearful determination, to persist still more obstinately in her assertions and her schemes.

There remained the third method: Klima could swear to the expectant mother that he had loved her once and loved her still. He should not make the slightest allusion to the chance that it was another man's child. On the contrary, Klima would bathe her in trust, tenderness, and love. He would promise her everything, including a divorce from his wife. He would depict their marvelous future together. And in behalf of that future he would then urge her to terminate the pregnancy. He would explain that this was not yet the time to have a child, that its birth would deprive them of the first, most beautiful years of their love.

This line of argument lacked what the preceding ones had in abundance: logic. How could Klima be so smitten with the nurse if he had been avoiding her for two months? But the bass player maintained that lovers always behaved illogically and that there was nothing simpler than explaining this, one way or another, to the young woman. Eventually they all agreed that the third method was probably the most satisfactory, for it would appeal to the young woman's love for him, the only relative certainty in the situation.

6

They left the theater and scattered at the street corner, but the guitarist accompanied Klima to his door. He was the only one to disapprove of the proposed plan. This plan seemed to him unworthy of the band-leader he revered: "When you go to see a woman, arm yourself with a whip!" said he, quoting the one sentence he knew of Nietzsche's collected works.

"My boy," Klima lamented, "she's the one with the whip."

The guitarist offered to go with Klima to the spa, lure the young woman out onto the road, and run her over: "Nobody could prove she didn't throw herself under my wheels."

The guitarist, the youngest musician in the group, greatly loved Klima, who was touched by his words: "That's very kind of you," he said to him.

The guitarist set out his plan in detail and with burning cheeks.

"That's very kind, but it's not possible," said Klima.

"Why are you hesitating? She's a slut!"

"You're really very kind, but it's not possible," said Klima, taking leave of the guitarist.

7

When he found himself alone, he thought about the young man's proposal and the reasons that had led him to reject it. It was not that he was more virtuous than the guitarist, but that he was more fearful. The fear of being accused as an accessory to murder was not less than the fear of being declared a father. He saw Ruzena run over by the car, he saw Ruzena stretched out on the road in a pool of blood, and he had a momentary feeling of relief that filled him with joy. But he knew it was useless to indulge in illusions. And he had a serious concern now. He thought of his wife. My God, tomorrow is her birthday!

It was a few minutes before six, and the shops would close at six exactly. He rushed into a florist's to buy a gigantic bouquet of roses. What a difficult celebration he expected! He would have to pretend to be near her in heart and mind, would have to give himself over to her, show tenderness to her, amuse her, laugh with her, and never for a moment stop thinking about a faraway belly. He would make an effort to utter affectionate words, but his mind would be far away, imprisoned in the dark cell of a stranger's womb.

He realized that it would be too much for him to spend this birthday at home, and he decided no longer to delay going to see Ruzena.

But this was not an agreeable prospect either. The mountain spa seemed like a desert to him. He knew no one there. Except perhaps for that American taking the waters, who, behaving like a rich bourgeois of the old days, had invited the whole group to his hotel suite after the concert. He had plied them with excellent drink and with women chosen from among the resort's staff, so that he was indirectly responsible for what happened afterward between Ruzena and Klima. Ah, if only that man, who had shown him such unreserved warmth, were still at the spa! Klima clung to his image as if to a last hope, for in moments such as those he was about to experience a man needs nothing more than the friendly understanding of another man.

He returned to the theater and stopped at the door-keeper's cubicle. He picked up the phone and asked for long distance. Soon he heard Ruzena's voice. He told her he would be coming to see her tomorrow. He made no reference to the news she had announced some hours before. He spoke to her as if they were carefree lovers.

In passing he asked: "Is the American still there?"

"Yes!" said Ruzena.

Feeling relieved, he repeated with somewhat more ease than before that he was greatly looking forward to seeing her. "What are you wearing?" he asked then.

"Why?"

This was a trick he had used successfully for years in telephone banter: "I want to know how you're dressed right now. I want to be able to imagine you."

"I'm wearing a red dress."

"Red must suit you very well."

"Could be," she said.

"And under your dress?"

She laughed.

Yes, they all laughed when they were asked this.

"What color are your underpants?"

"Also red."

"I'm looking forward to seeing you in them," he said, hanging up. He thought he had used the right tone. For a moment he felt better. But only for a moment. He quickly realized that he was actually incapable of thinking about anything but Ruzena, and that he would have to keep conversation with his wife this evening to the barest minimum. He stopped at the box office of a movie theater showing an American Western and bought two tickets.

8

Although she was much more beautiful than she was unhealthy, Kamila Klíma was nonetheless unhealthy. Because of her fragile health she had been forced, some years before, to give up the singing career that had led her into the arms of the man who was now her husband.

The beautiful young woman who had been accustomed to admiration suddenly had a head filled with the smell of hospital disinfectant. It seemed to her that between her husband's world and her own a mountain range had sprung up.

At that time, when Klíma saw her sad face, he felt his heart break and (across that imaginary mountain range) he held loving hands out to her. Kamila realized that in her sadness there was a hitherto unsuspected force that attracted Klíma, softened him, brought tears to his eyes. It was no surprise that she began to make use (perhaps unconsciously, but all the more often) of this unexpectedly discovered tool. For it was only when he was gazing at her sorrowful face that she could be more or less certain no other woman was competing with her in Klima's mind.

· This very beautiful woman was actually afraid of women and saw them everywhere. Nowhere could they escape her. She knew how to find them in Klima's intonation when he greeted her upon arriving home. She knew how to detect them from the smell of his clothes. Recently she had found a scrap of newspaper; a date was written on it in Klima's handwriting. Of course it could have referred to any one of a variety of events— a concert rehearsal, a meeting with an impresario—but for a whole month she did nothing but wonder which woman Klima was going to meet that day, and for a whole month she slept badly.

If the treacherous world of women frightened her so, could she not find solace in the world of men?

Hardly. Jealousy has the amazing power to illuminate a single person in an intense beam of light, keeping the multitude of others in total darkness. Mrs. Klima's thoughts could go only in the direction of that painful beam, and her husband became the only man in the world.

Now she heard the key in the lock, and then she saw the trumpeter with a bouquet of roses.

· At first she felt pleased, but doubts immediately arose: Why was he bringing her flowers this evening, when her birthday was not until tomorrow? What could this mean?

And she greeted him by saying: "Won't you be here tomorrow?"

9

Bringing her roses this evening did not necessarily imply he was going to be away tomorrow. But her distrustful antennae, eternally vigilant, eternally jealous, could pick up her husband's slightest secret intention well in advance. Whenever Klima noticed those terrible antennae spying on him, unmasking him, stripping him naked, he was overcome by a hopeless sensation of fatigue. He hated those antennae, and he was sure that if his marriage was under threat, it was from them. He had always been convinced (and on this point with a belligerently clear conscience) that he deceived his wife only because he wanted to spare her, to shelter her from any anxiety, and that her own suspicions were what made her suffer.

He gazed at her face, reading on it suspicion, sadness, and a bad mood. He felt like throwing the bouquet of roses on the floor, but he controlled himself. He knew that in the next few days he would have to control himself in much more difficult situations.

"Does it bother you that I brought you flowers this evening?" he said. Sensing the irritation in his voice, his wife thanked him and went to fill a vase with water.

"That damned socialism!" Klima said next.

"What now?"

"Listen! They're always making us play for nothing. One time it's for the struggle against imperialism, another time it's to commemorate the revolution, still another time it's for some big shot's birthday, and if I want to keep the band going, I have to agree to everything. You can't imagine how they got to me today."

"What was it?" she asked indifferently.

"The president of the Municipal Council turned up at rehearsal and she started telling us what we should play and what we shouldn't play and finally forced us to schedule a free concert for the Youth League. But the worst part is I'll have to spend all day tomorrow at a ridiculous conference where they're going to talk to us about the role of music in building socialism. One more day wasted, totally wasted! And right on your birthday!"

"They won't really keep you there all evening!"

"Probably not. But you can see what a state I'll be in when I come home! So I thought we could spend some quiet time together this evening," he said, taking hold of his wife's hands.

"That's nice of you," said Mrs. Klima, and Klima realized from her tone of voice that she didn't believe a word of what he had said about tomorrow's conference. Of course she didn't dare show him she didn't believe him. She knew her distrust would infuriate him. But Klima had long ago stopped believing in his wife's credulity. Whether he told the truth or lied, he always suspected her of suspecting him. Yet the die was cast; he had to keep on pretending to believe she believed him, and she (with a sad, strange face) asked questions about tomorrow's conference to show him she had no doubt of its reality.

Then she went to the kitchen to prepare dinner. She used too much salt. She liked to cook and was very good at it (life had not spoiled her, she had not lost the habit of housekeeping), and Klima knew that the cause of the evening's unsuccessful meal could only have been her distress. He saw her in his mind's eye making the pained, violent movement of pouring an excessive amount of salt into the food, and it wrung his heart. It seemed to him that with every oversalted mouthful he was tasting Kamila's tears, and it was his own guilt that he was swallowing. He knew Kamila was tormented by jealousy, he knew she would spend still another sleepless night, and he wanted to caress her, embrace her, soothe her, but he instantly realized it would be useless, because in this tenderness his wife's antennae would only pick up proof of his bad conscience.

Finally they went to the movie theater. Klima drew some comfort from the sight of the hero on the screen escaping treacherous dangers with infectious self-assurance. He imagined himself in the hero's shoes and now and then felt that persuading Ruzena to have an abortion would be a trifle that could be accomplished in a flash, thanks to his charm and his lucky star.

Later they lay side by side in the big bed. He looked at her. She was on her back, her head sunk into the pillow, her chin slightly raised, her eyes fixed on the ceiling, and in her body's extreme tension (it had always made him think of a violin, and he would tell her she had "the soul of a taut string") he suddenly experienced, in a single instant, her entire essence. Yes, it sometimes happened (these were miraculous moments) that he could suddenly grasp, in a single one of her gestures or movements, the entire history of her body and soul. These were moments of absolute clairvoyance but also of absolute emotion; for the woman who had loved him when he was still a nobody, who had been ready to sacrifice everything for him, who so understood his thoughts that he could talk to her about Armstrong or Stravinsky, about trivial and serious things, she was closer to him than any other human being. . . . Then he imagined that this lovely body, this lovely face, was dead, and he felt he would be unable to survive her by a single day. He knew that he was capable of protecting her to his last breath, that he was capable of giving his life for her.

But this stifling sensation of love was merely a feeble fleeting glimmer, because his mind was wholly preoccupied by anxiety and fear. He lay beside Kamila, he knew he loved her boundlessly, but he was absent mentally. He caressed her face as if he were caressing it from an immeasurable distance some hundreds of kilometers away.

Second Day

1

It was about nine in the morning in the spa town when an elegant white sedan pulled up in the parking lot at the edge of the spa proper (automobiles were not permitted any farther) and Klima stepped out of it.

Running through the spa was a long, narrow park with scattered clusters of trees, sand paths, and colorful benches on the lawn. Along both sides of the park stood the thermal center's buildings, among them Karl Marx House, where the trumpeter had spent a couple of fateful hours one night in Nurse Ruzena's little room. Facing Karl Marx House on the other side of the park was the spa's most handsome structure, a building in the turn-of-the-century art nouveau style covered with stucco embellishments and with broad steps leading up to the entrance and a mosaic over it. It alone had been accorded the privilege of keeping its original name: Hotel Richmond.

"Is Mister Bertlef still staying here?" Klima asked at the desk, and, receiving an affirmative reply, he ran up the red-carpeted stairs to the second floor and knocked at a door.

Upon entering he saw Bertlef, who came to meet him in his pajamas. Embarrassed, Klima started to apologize for his unexpected visit, but Bertlef interrupted: "My friend! Don't apologize! You are giving me the greatest pleasure I have ever had here so early in the day."

He gripped Klima's hand and went on: "In this country people don't respect the morning. An alarm clock violently wakes them up, shatters their sleep like the blow of an ax, and they immediately surrender themselves to deadly haste. Can you tell me what kind of day can follow a beginning of such violence? What happens to people whose alarm clock daily gives them a small electric shock? Each day they become more used to violence and less used to pleasure. Believe me, it is the mornings that determine a man's character."

Bertlef took Klima gently by the shoulder, steered him to an armchair, and went on: "And to think that I so love those morning hours of idleness when, as if over a bridge lined with statues, I slowly go across from night to day, from sleep to awakened life. This is the time of day when I would be so very grateful for a small miracle, for an unexpected encounter that would convince me that my nocturnal dreams are continuing, that no chasm separates the adventures of sleep from the adventures of the day."

As the trumpeter watched Bertlef pacing up and down the room in his pajamas and smoothing his graying hair with his hand, he heard in the sonorous voice an ineradicable American accent and something charmingly outdated about his vocabulary, which was easily explained by Bertlef's never having lived here in his family's country of origin and having learned its language only from his parents.

"And no one, my friend," he now explained, leaning over Klima with a confiding smile, "no one in this entire spa understands me. Even the nurses, who are otherwise quite obliging, look indignant when I invite them to share a bit of pleasant time with me during breakfast, so I must postpone such appointments until the evening, when I am really a little tired."

Then he went over to a small telephone table and asked: "When did you arrive?"

"This morning," said Klima. "I drove."

"You are surely hungry," said Bertlef, and he picked up the receiver. He ordered two breakfasts: "Four poached eggs, cheese, butter, rolls, milk, ham, and tea."

Meanwhile Klima scrutinized the room. A large round table, chairs, an armchair, a mirror, two couches, and doors leading to the bathroom and, he remembered, to Bertlef's small bedroom. Here in this luxurious suite was where it had all started. Here had sat the tipsy musicians of his band, for whose pleasure the rich American had invited some nurses.

"Yes," said Bertlef, "the picture you are looking at was not here before."

It was only then that the trumpeter noticed a canvas showing a bearded man with a strange, pale-blue disk behind his head and holding a paintbrush and a palette. The picture seemed ineptly done, but the trumpeter knew that many seemingly inept pictures were famous works of art.

"Who painted that?"

"I did," replied Bertlef.

"I didn't know you painted."

"I love to paint."

"And who is this?" the trumpeter was emboldened to ask.

"Saint Lazarus."

"What do you mean? Was Lazarus a painter?"

"This is not the Lazarus in the Bible, but Saint Lazarus, a monk who lived in the ninth century in Constantinople. He is my patron saint."

"Really!" said the trumpeter.

"He was a very odd saint. He was not martyred by pagans because he believed in Christ, but by wicked Christians because he loved painting too much. As you may know, in the eighth and ninth centuries the Greek Orthodox Church fell prey to a rigorous asceticism intolerant of all worldly joys. Even paintings and statues were considered objects of impious pleasure. The emperor Theophilus ordered thousands of beautiful paintings destroyed and prohibited my cherished Lazarus from painting. But Lazarus knew that his paintings glorified God, and he refused to yield. Theophilus threw him into prison, had him tortured, demanded that Lazarus give up painting, but God was merciful and gave him the strength to bear cruel ordeals."

"That's a beautiful story," said the trumpeter politely.

"A magnificent one. But surely it was not to look at

my paintings that you came here to see me."

Just then there was a knock at the door, and a waiter came in with a large tray. He set it on the table and laid out breakfast for the two men.

Bertlef asked the trumpeter to sit down at the table and said: "This breakfast is not remarkable enough to keep us from continuing our conversation. Tell me, what is on your mind?"

And so, as he chewed, the trumpeter told of his misfortune, prompting Bertlef at various points of the story to come up with penetrating questions.

2

He wanted above all to know why Klima had not answered the nurse's two postcards, why he had not taken her telephone calls, and why he had never made a single friendly gesture that might have prolonged their night of love with a quiet, calming echo.

Klima acknowledged that his behavior had been neither gracious nor sensible. But, so he said, it was all too much for him. He had a horror of any further contact with the young woman.

"Any fool can seduce a woman," Bertlef said with annoyance. "But one must also know how to break it off; that is the sign of a mature man."

"I know," the trumpeter admitted sadly, "but my loathing, my absolute distaste, is stronger than all my good intentions."

"Tell me," Bertlef said with surprise, "are you a misogynist?"

"That's what they say about me."

"But how is that possible? You don't seem to be impotent or homosexual."

"That's right, I'm neither. It's something much worse," the trumpeter admitted melancholically. "I love my wife. That's my erotic secret, which most people find totally incomprehensible."

This confession was so moving that both men kept silent for a while. Then the trumpeter went on: "Nobody understands this, my wife least of all. She thinks that a great love keeps us from having affairs. But that's a mistake. Something's always pushing me toward some other woman, and yet once I've had her I'm torn away by a powerful spring that catapults me back to Kamila. I sometimes feel that I look for other women only because of that spring, that momentum, that marvelous flight—filled with tenderness, desire, humility—bringing me back to my wife, whom I love even more with every new infidelity."

"So for you Nurse Ruzena is only a way of confirming your monogamous love."

"Yes," said the trumpeter. "And it's an extremely pleasant confirmation. Ruzena has great charm at first sight, and also it's an advantage that her charm totally fades away in two hours, which means that there's nothing urging you to go on with it, and that spring launches you into a marvelous return flight."

"Dear friend, excessive love is guilty love, and you are certainly the best proof of it."

"I thought my love for my wife was the only good thing about me."

"And you were wrong. The excessive love you bear your wife is not the opposite pole to your insensitivity, it is its source. Because your wife means everything to you, all other women mean nothing to you; in other words, for you they are whores. But this is great blasphemy, great contempt for creatures made by God. My dear friend, that kind of love is heresy."

3

Bertlef pushed aside his empty cup, got up from the table, and retired to the bathroom, from which Klima first heard the sound of running water and then, after a moment, Bertlef's voice: "Do you think one has the right to put to death a child that has not yet seen the light of day?"

A while ago he had been discomfited by the portrait of the bearded man with the halo. He had remembered Bertlef as a jovial bon vivant, and it would never have occurred to him that the man could be a believer. He felt a pang of anxiety at the thought that he was going to be getting a lesson in morality and that his sole oasis in this desert of a spa was going to be covered with sand. He replied in a choked voice: "Are you one of those who calls that murder?"

Bertlef delayed answering. When he finally emerged from the bathroom, he was dressed to go out and meticulously combed.

"'Murder' is a word that smacks a little too much of the electric chair," he said. "That is not what I am trying to say. You know, I am convinced that life must be accepted such as it is given to us. That is the real first commandment, prior to the other ten. All events are in the hands of God, and we know nothing about their evolution. I am trying to say that to accept life such as it is given to us is to accept the unforeseeable. And a child is the quintessence of the unforeseeable. A child is unforeseeability itself. You don't know what it will become, what it will bring you, and that is precisely why you must accept it. Otherwise you are only half alive, you are living like a nonswimmer wading near the shore, while the ocean is not really the ocean until you are out of your depth."

The trumpeter pointed out that the child was not his.

"Let us assume that that is so," said Bertlef. "But you in turn should frankly admit that if the child were yours you would be just as persistent in trying to convince Ruzena to have an abortion. You would be doing it for the sake of your wife and of your guilty love for her."

"Yes, I admit it," said the trumpeter. "I'd insist she have an abortion under any circumstances."

Still leaning against the bathroom door, Bertlef smiled: "I understand you, and I shall not attempt to make you change your mind. I am too old to want to improve the world. I have told you what I think, and that is all. I shall remain your friend even if you act contrary to my convictions, and I shall help you even if I disagree with you."

The trumpeter scrutinized Bertlef, who uttered these last words in the velvety voice of a wise preacher. He found him admirable. He felt that everything Bertlef said could be a legend, a parable, an example, a chapter from a modern gospel. He wanted (we should know that he was moved by and drawn to inflated gestures) to bow down before him.

"I shall do my best to help you," Bertlef went on. "In a while we are going to see my friend Doctor Skreta, who will settle the medical aspect of the matter. But tell me, how are you going to induce Ruzena to do something she is reluctant to do?"

4

When the trumpeter had presented his plan, Bertlef said: "This reminds me of something that happened to me in my adventurous youth, when I was working on the docks as a longshoreman, and there was a girl there who brought us our lunch. She had an exceptionally kind heart and didn't know how to refuse anyone anything. Alas, such kindness of heart—and body—makes men more crude than grateful, so that I was the only one to pay her any respectful attention, although I was also the only one who had not gone to bed with her. Because of my gentleness she fell in love with me. It would have hurt and humiliated her if I had not made love to her. But this happened only once, and I immediately explained to her that I would go on loving her with a great spiritual love, but that we could no longer be lovers. She burst into tears, she ran off, she stopped talking to me, and she gave herself still more conspicuously to all the others. When two months had gone by, she told me she was pregnant by me."

"So you were in the same situation I'm in!" the trumpeter exclaimed.

"Ah, my friend," said Bertlef, "are you not aware that what has happened to you is every man's lot?"

"And what did you do?"

"I behaved exactly as you are planning to behave, but with one difference. You are going to try to pretend to love Ruzena, whereas I really loved that girl. I saw before me a poor creature humiliated and insulted by everyone, a poor creature to whom only a single being in the world had ever shown any consideration, and this consideration was something she did not want to lose. I realized that she loved me, and I just could not hold it against her that she showed it the only way she could, the way provided her by her innocent low-mindedness. Listen to what I told her: 'I know very well that you are pregnant by someone else. But I also know that you are employing this ruse out of love, and I want to repay your love with my love. I don't care whose child it is, if it is your wish, I shall marry you.'"

"That was crazy!"

"But probably more effective than your carefully prepared maneuver. After I had told the little tart many times that I loved her and wanted to marry her and keep the child, she dissolved in tears and confessed she had lied to me. My kindness made her realize, she said, that she was not worthy of me, that she could never marry me."

The trumpeter remained silent and pensive, and Bertlef added: "I would be glad if this story could serve you as a parable. Don't try to make Ruzena believe you love her, try truly to love her. Try to feel pity for her. Even if she misled you, try to see in this lie a form of her love. I am certain she will then be unable to withstand the power of your kindness, and she herself will make all the arrangements required to avoid wronging you."

Bertlef's words made a great impression on the trumpeter. But as soon as Ruzena had come to mind in a more vivid light, he realized that the path of love, which Bertlef had suggested, was closed to him; it was the path of saints, not of ordinary men.

5

Ruzena was sitting at a small table in the huge room in the thermal building where, after undergoing treatment, women rested in beds lined up against the walls. She had just received the charts of two new patients. She filled in the date and gave the women towels, large white sheets, and keys to the changing cubicles. Then she looked at her watch and headed for the adjoining room (she was wearing only a white smock over her bare body, because the tiled rooms were filled with hot steam), to the pool where some twenty naked women were splashing about in the miraculous spring waters. She called three of them by name, to tell them their time was up. The ladies obediently left the pool, shaking their bulky, dripping breasts and following Ruzena, who escorted them back to the treatment room to lie down on vacant beds. One after another, she wrapped each in a sheet, wiped each one's eyes with a bit of it, and covered her with a warm blanket. The ladies gave her a smile, but Ruzena didn't smile in return.

It is surely not pleasant to have been born in a small town through which every year ten thousand women but practically no young men pass; unless she moves elsewhere, a woman will have a precise idea by the age of fifteen of all the erotic possibilities her lifetime will offer her. And how is she to move elsewhere? Her employers did not readily release their employees, and

Ruzena's parents protested vehemently whenever she hinted at moving away.

No, this young woman, who all in all did her best to fulfill her professional obligations meticulously, felt no great love for the women taking the waters. We can cite three reasons for this:

Envy: These women came here directly from husbands and lovers, from a world she imagined teeming with a thousand possibilities inaccessible to her, even though she had prettier breasts, longer legs, and more regular features.

Besides envy, impatience: These women came here with their destinies far away, and she was here without a destiny, with one year the same as the next; she was frightened by the thought that, in this small town, she was living an eventless time span, and, despite her youth, constantly thought that life was passing her by before she had begun to live.

Third, there was the instinctive dislike inspired in her by their sheer numbers, which diminished each woman's worth as an individual. She was surrounded by a sad excess of bosoms, among which even a bosom as attractive as hers lost its worth.

Without a smile, she had just wrapped the last of three women when her thin colleague stuck her head into the room and shouted: "Ruzena! Telephone!"

Her colleague's expression was so reverent that Ruzena knew at once who had phoned her. Blushing, she went behind the cubicles, picked up the receiver, and gave her name.

Klima identified himself and asked her when she would be free to see him.

"I finish work at three. We could see each other at four."

Then they had to agree on where to meet. Ruzena suggested the spa's big brasserie, which was open all day. The thin nurse, who was standing beside Ruzena and keeping her eyes fixed on her lips, gave an approving nod. The trumpeter replied that he preferred to see Ruzena in a place where they could be alone and suggested driving out into the country in his car.

"What for? Where would we go?"

"We'd be alone."

"If you're ashamed of me you shouldn't have bothered to come here," said Ruzena, and her colleague nodded.

"That's not what I meant," said Klima. "I'll meet you at four in front of the brasserie."

"Perfect," said the thin nurse when Ruzena hung up. "He wants to meet you in some hideaway, but you have to make sure you're seen together by as many people as possible."

Ruzena was still very agitated, and the prospect of the meeting made her nervous. She could no longer picture Klima. What did his face, his smile, his posture look like? Their single encounter had left her only a vague memory. Her colleagues had pressed her at the time with questions about the trumpeter, they wanted to know what he was like, what he said, what he looked like undressed, and how he made love. But she was unable to tell them anything, and merely repeated that it was "like a dream."

This was not simply a cliché: the man with whom she had spent two hours in bed had come down from the posters to join her. For a moment his photograph had acquired a three-dimensional reality, a warmth, a weight, and then had again become an impalpable, colorless image reproduced in thousands of copies and thus all the more abstract and unreal.

And because he had then so quickly escaped back into being his own graphic sign, his icon, she had been left with an unpleasant awareness of his perfection. She was unable to cling to a single detail that would bring him down or bring him nearer. When he was far away, she had been full of energetic combativeness, but now that she felt his presence, her courage failed her.

"Hang in there," said the thin nurse. "I'll keep my fingers crossed."

6

When Klima had finished his phone conversation with Ruzena, Bertlef took him by the arm and led him across the park to Karl Marx House, where Dr. Skreta had his office and living quarters. Several women were sitting in the waiting room, but Bertlef without hesitation rapped sharply four times on the office door. In an instant a tall man appeared, wearing a white coat and with eyeglasses on his big nose. "Just a moment, please," he said to the women sitting in the waiting room, and then he led the two men into the corridor and up the stairs to his apartment on the floor above.

"How are you, Maestro?" he said, addressing the trumpeter when all three were seated. "When are you going to give another concert here?"

"Never again in my lifetime," answered Klima, "because this spa jinxed me."

Bertlef explained to Dr. Skreta what had happened to the trumpeter, and then Klima added: "I want to ask for your help. First, I want to know if she's really pregnant. Maybe she's just late. Or it's all an act. That's already happened to me once. That one was a blonde too."

"Never start anything with a blonde," said Dr. Skreta.

"Yes," Klima agreed, "blondes are my downfall. Doctor, it was horrible that time. I had her examined by a physician. But at the beginning of a pregnancy you can't tell anything for sure. So I insisted they do the mouse test. The one where they inject urine into a mouse and if the mouse's ovaries swell up . . ."

". . . the lady is pregnant," Dr. Skreta finished.

"She was carrying her morning urine in a little bottle, I was with her, and right in front of the clinic she dropped the little bottle on the sidewalk. I pounced on those bits of glass trying to save at least a few drops! Seeing me, you'd have sworn I'd dropped the Holy Grail. She did it on purpose, broke the little bottle, because she knew she wasn't pregnant and she wanted to make my ordeal last as long as possible."

"Typical blonde behavior," Dr. Skreta said, unsurprised.

"Do you think there is a difference between blondes and brunettes?" asked Bertlef, visibly skeptical about Dr. Skreta's experience with women.

"You bet!" said Dr. Skreta. "Blonde hair and black hair are the two poles of human nature. Black hair signifies virility, courage, frankness, activity, while blonde hair symbolizes femininity, tenderness, weakness, and passivity. Therefore a blonde is in fact doubly a woman. A princess can only be blonde. That's also why, to be as feminine as possible, women dye their hair yellow but never black."

"I'm curious about how pigments exercise their influence over the human soul," said Bertlef doubtfully.

"It's not a matter of pigments. A blonde unconsciously adapts herself to her hair. Especially if the blonde is a brunette who dyes her hair yellow. She tries to be faithful to her hair color and behaves like a fragile creature, a shallow doll, she demands tenderness and service, courtesy and alimony, she's incapable of doing anything for herself, all refinement on the outside and coarseness on the inside. If black hair became a universal fashion, life in this world would clearly be better. It would be the most useful social reform ever achieved."

"So it's very likely that Ruzena is also putting on an act," Klima interjected, looking for hope in Dr. Skreta's words.

"No. I examined her yesterday. She's pregnant," said the physician.

Bertlef noticed that the trumpeter had gone pale, and he said: "Doctor, you are chairman of the Abortion Committee here, are you not?"

"Yes," said Dr. Skreta. "We're meeting on Friday."

"Perfect," said Bertlef. "There is no time to lose, because our friend is having a breakdown. I realize that in this country you don't readily authorize abortions."

"Not at all readily," said Dr. Skreta. "On the committee with me are two females who are there to represent the power of the people. They're repulsively ugly and hate all the women who come before us. Do you know who are the most virulent misogynists in the world? Women. No man, gentlemen, not even Mister Klima, whom two women have already attempted to hold responsible for their pregnancies, has ever felt such hatred for women as women themselves feel toward their own sex. Why do you think they try to seduce us? Solely to defy and humiliate their fellow women. God instilled in women's hearts a hatred of other women because He wanted the human race to multiply."

"I shall forgive this remark of yours," said Bertlef,

"because I want to return to our friend's problem. Aren't you really the one who makes the decisions on that committee, and those hideous females do whatever you say?"

"I'm certainly the one who decides, but this doesn't mean I want to keep on doing it. It pays nothing. Tell me, Maestro, how much are you paid, for example, for one concert?"

The amount mentioned by Klima interested Dr. Skreta: "I often think I could supplement my income by making music. I'm not a bad drummer."

"You're a drummer?" asked Klima, showing forced interest.

"Yes," said Dr. Skreta. "We have a piano and a set of drums in the Hall of the People. I play the drums in my free moments."

"That's wonderful!" exclaimed the trumpeter, pleased by the opportunity to flatter the physician.

"But I don't have any partners to have a real band with. There's only the pharmacist, who plays the piano fairly well. We've tried out some things together a few times." He broke off and seemed to be thinking. "Listen! When Ruzena appears before the committee . . ."

Klima gave a deep sigh. "If she would only come—"

Dr. Skreta gestured impatiently: "She'll be glad to come, just like all the others. But the committee requires the father to appear too; you'll have to be there with her. And to make the trip here worthwhile, you might arrive the day before and give a concert that evening. Trumpet, piano, drums. *Tres faciunt*

43

orchestrum. With your name on the posters, we'll fill the hall. What do you say?"

Klima was always excessively punctilious about the technical quality of his concerts, and two days earlier the physician's proposal would have seemed completely insane to him. But now he was only interested in a particular nurse's womb, and he responded to the physician's question with polite enthusiasm: "That would be splendid!"

"Really? Will you do it?"

"Of course."

"And you, what do you say?" Skreta asked Bertlef.

"It seems an excellent idea to me. But I don't know how you can make all the preparations in two days."

By way of response, Skreta got up and went over to the phone. He dialed a number, but there was no answer. "The most important thing is to order the posters right away. Unfortunately the secretary must have gone to lunch," he said. "Getting the use of the hall is child's play. The People's Education Association has an anti-alcohol meeting scheduled for Thursday, and one of my colleagues is supposed to give the lecture. He'll be delighted when I ask him to cancel because of illness. But of course you'll have to get here on Thursday morning so the three of us can rehearse. Unless it's unnecessary."

"No, no," said Klima. "It's essential. You have to prepare in advance."

"That's my opinion too," said Skreta. "Let's play them the most surefire program. I'm good at backing up 'St. Louis Blues' and 'When the Saints Go Marching In.' I've got some solos ready, I'm curious to know what you'll think of them. For that matter, are you free this afternoon? Would you like to give it a try?"

"Unfortunately, this afternoon I have to persuade Ruzena to consent to an abortion."

Skreta waved his hand: "Forget about that! She'll consent without any coaxing."

"Doctor," Klima pleaded, "better on Thursday."

Bertlef interceded: "I too think you would do better to wait until Thursday. Today our friend would be unable to concentrate. Anyway, I don't believe he has brought his trumpet with him."

"That's a good reason!" Skreta acknowledged, and began to lead his two friends to the restaurant on the other side of the park. But Skreta's nurse caught up with them and begged him to return to his office. The doctor excused himself and let the nurse take him back to his infertile patients.

7

About six months earlier Ruzena had left her parents' house in a nearby village to move into a small room in Karl Marx House. God knows what she promised herself from this room's independence, but she soon realized that her room's and her freedom's benefits were much less pleasant and much less intense than what she had dreamed of.

This afternoon, having returned to her room from the thermal building a little after three o'clock, she had the unpleasant surprise of finding her father waiting for her sprawled on the daybed. That was hardly convenient, for she wanted to devote herself entirely to her appearance, to do her hair and carefully choose a dress.

"What are you doing here?" she asked irritably. She held it against the doorkeeper that he was an acquaintance of her father's and always ready to let him into her room in her absence.

"I had a bit of free time," said her father. "We're having an exercise in town today."

Her father was a member of the Public Order Volunteers. Because the spa's medical staff made fun of the old men pacing up and down the streets with their armbands and their self-important manner, Ruzena was ashamed of this activity of her father's.

"If that's what amuses you!" she muttered.

"You should be glad to have a papa who's never been a loafer and never will be. We're pensioners, but we're going to show you young people we still know how to do things!"

Ruzena decided to let him talk while she concentrated on choosing her dress. She opened the wardrobe.

"I'd really like to know what things you do," she said.

"A lot of things. This town, my little girl, is an

internationally known spa. And what do you see? Kids running all over the grass!"

"So what?" said Ruzena, rummaging through her dresses. Not a single one pleased her.

"Not only kids, but dogs too! The Municipal Council a long time ago issued an order that dogs have to be leashed and muzzled outdoors! But nobody here obeys it. Everybody does what he pleases. Just look at the park!"

Ruzena took out a dress and began to change behind the open wardrobe door.

"They piss everywhere. Even in the playground sandbox! Think of a toddler dropping his slice of bread and jam in the sand! And then people wonder why there's so much sickness! Here, all you have to do is look," said her father, heading toward the window. "Right now four dogs are running loose there."

Ruzena reappeared and examined herself in the mirror on the wall. The little mirror was the only one she had, and she could barely see down to her waist.

"You're not interested, are you?" her father asked.

"Of course I'm interested," said Ruzena, moving back from the mirror on tiptoes to try to gauge how her legs would look in that dress. "But, please don't be angry, I've got to meet somebody and I'm in a hurry."

"The only dogs I can tolerate are police dogs and retrievers," said her father. "But I don't understand people who keep dogs at home. Soon women will stop bearing children and cradles will be filled with poodles!"

Ruzena was dissatisfied with the image the mirror reflected. She went back to the wardrobe to find a more becoming dress.

"We've decided that people should be allowed to have dogs at home only if everybody in the building agrees to it at the tenants' meeting. Also, we're going to increase the dog-license fee."

"I can see you have serious concerns," said Ruzena, delighted that she no longer lived with her parents. Ever since childhood, her father's moral lessons and commands had been repugnant to her. She craved a world in which people spoke a language other than his.

"It's no laughing matter. Dogs really are a serious problem, and I'm not the only one who thinks so, the highest authorities think so too. You've probably never been asked what's important and what isn't. Of course you'd answer that the most important things in the world are your dresses," he said, noting that his daughter had again hidden behind the wardrobe door to change.

"They're certainly more important than your dogs," she replied, once again standing on tiptoes in front of the mirror. And once again she was dissatisfied. But dissatisfaction with herself slowly changed into rebellion: spitefully she thought that the trumpeter would have to accept her just as she was, even in this cheap dress, and this gave her an odd feeling of satisfaction.

"It's a question of hygiene," her father went on. "Our towns will never be clean as long as dogs leave their loads on the sidewalk. And it's also a question of morality. It's intolerable for dogs to be pampered in housing constructed for people."

Something was happening that Ruzena did not suspect: her rebellion was mysteriously, imperceptibly merging with her father's indignation. She no longer felt the intense repugnance for him that had filled her just a while ago; on the contrary, she unknowingly drew energy from his vehement words.

"We never had a dog in the house, and we weren't missing anything," said her father.

She continued to look at herself in the mirror and felt that being pregnant gave her a new advantage. Whether she found herself beautiful or not, the trumpeter had made the trip expressly to see her and very nicely invited her to meet him at the brasserie. For that matter (she looked at her watch), at this very moment he was already waiting for her there.

"But we're going to make a clean sweep, little girl, you'll see!" her father said, laughing, and this time she reacted gently, almost with a smile: "I'm glad, Papa. But now I have to leave."

"Me too. The exercise starts again any minute."

They left Karl Marx House together and then went their separate ways. Ruzena headed slowly toward the brasserie.

8

Klima had never managed to identify entirely with his role of a famous and popular artist, and particularly now, with his private worries, he felt it as a flaw and a handicap. When he entered the brasserie with Ruzena and, opposite the checkroom, saw his enlarged photo on a poster left over from the last concert, he was gripped by a sensation of anxiety. He crossed the room with the young woman, automatically trying to guess which of the customers recognized him. He was afraid of their gaze, thought he saw eyes everywhere observing him, spying on him, dictating his expressions and behavior to him. He felt several curious looks fixed on him. He tried to ignore them and headed for a small table in the back, near a bay window with a view of the park's foliage.

When they were seated he smiled at Ruzena, caressed her hand, and said that her dress became her. She demurred modestly, but he insisted and tried to talk for a while on the topic of the nurse's charms. He was surprised, he said, by her good looks. He had been thinking about her so much for two months that the pictorial efforts of his memory had fashioned an image of her that was remote from the reality. What was extraordinary about it, he said, was that her real appearance, although he had very much desired it as he thought of her, nonetheless topped the imaginary one.

Ruzena pointed out that she had not heard from the trumpeter for two months, and from that she gathered that he had not thought of her very much.

This was an objection he had carefully prepared for. He sighed wearily and told the young woman she could have no idea of the terrible two months he had just spent. Ruzena asked him what had happened, but the trumpeter didn't want to go into the details. He merely replied that he had been the victim of great ingratitude and had suddenly found himself all alone in the world, without friends, without anyone.

He was a little afraid that Ruzena would start questioning him in detail about his worries, with the risk of his becoming entangled in lies. His fears were excessive. Ruzena was of course very interested to learn that the trumpeter had gone through a difficult time, and she readily accepted this excuse for his two-month silence. But she was completely indifferent to the exact nature of his troubles. About those sad months he had just lived through, only the sadness interested her.

"I thought a lot about you, and it would have made me so happy to help you."

"I was so disgusted I was even afraid to see people. Sad company is bad company."

"I was sad too."

"I know," he said, caressing her hand.

"I've known for quite a while that I'm carrying your child. And you gave no sign of life. But I'd have kept the child even if you never wanted to see me again. I told myself that even if I'm left all alone, I'll at least have your child. I'd never get rid of it. No, never . . ."

Klima was speechless; mute terror took hold of his mind.

Fortunately for him the waiter, who was casual about serving the customers, now stopped at their table for their order.

"A brandy," said the trumpeter, and immediately corrected himself: "Two brandies."

There was another pause, and Ruzena repeated in an undertone: "No, not for anything in the world would I ever get rid of it."

"Don't say that," Klima replied, regaining his wits. "You're not the only one involved. A child is not only the woman's business. It's the couple's business. Both of them have to agree, or else things could end very badly."

When he finished he realized he had just indirectly admitted that he was the child's father. From now on any conversation with Ruzena would be based on that admission. He was well aware that he was acting according to plan and that this concession was part of it, yet he was terrified of his own words.

The waiter brought them the two brandies: "Are you really Mister Klima, the trumpet player?"

"Yes," said Klima.

"The girls in the kitchen recognized you. That's really you on the poster?"

"Yes," said Klima.

"It seems you're the idol of all the women between twelve and seventy!" said the waiter, adding for

Ruzena's benefit: "All the women are so envious they want to scratch your eyes out!" As he left he turned around several times to smile at them with impertinent familiarity.

"No, I'll never agree to get rid of it," Ruzena repeated. "And you too, someday, you'll be happy to have it. Because, you understand, I'm not asking you for anything at all. I hope you don't imagine I want something from you. You can absolutely set your mind at rest. This concerns only me, and if you wish, you don't have to deal with any of it."

Nothing makes a man more anxious than such reassurances. Klima suddenly felt that he had no strength left to salvage anything at all and that he had better give up the game. He was silent and Ruzena was silent too, and the words she had just spoken became so rooted in the silence that the trumpeter felt more and more miserable and helpless in their presence.

But the image of his wife suddenly came to mind. He realized that he must not give up. He moved his hand on the marble tabletop until it touched Ruzena's fingers. He gripped them and said: "Forget about the child for a minute. The child is not at all the most important thing. Do you think we don't have anything to say to each other about the two of us? Do you think I came to see you only because of the child?"

Ruzena shrugged.

"The most important thing is that I feel sad without you. We saw each other only for a brief moment. And yet there wasn't a single day that I didn't think of you."

He paused, and Ruzena remarked: "I never heard from you for two months, and I wrote to you twice."

"Don't hold it against me," said the trumpeter. "It was on purpose that you didn't hear from me. I didn't want to be in touch with you. I was afraid of what was happening inside me. I was resisting love. I wished to write you a long letter, I actually filled pages and pages, but I finally threw them all away. I was never so in love before, and it scared me. And why not admit it? I also wanted to make sure that my feelings were something other than a passing enchantment. I told myself: If I go on being like this for another month, what I'm feeling for her isn't an illusion, it's a reality."

Ruzena said softly: "And what do you think now? Is it only an illusion?"

When Ruzena said this, the trumpeter realized that his plan was beginning to work. So he kept holding her hand and went on talking, the words coming more and more easily to him: Now that he was here looking at her, he said, he realized it wouldn't be necessary to submit his feelings to any more tests because everything was clear. And he didn't wish to speak of the child because most important to him was not the child but Ruzena. The significance of the child she was carrying was precisely that of having called him, Klima, to Ruzena's side. Yes, the child she was carrying inside her had called him here to this small spa and made him see how much he loved Ruzena, and that was why (he raised his glass of brandy) they were going to drink to the child's health.

Of course he was instantly frightened by the appalling toast to which his verbal exhilaration had brought him. But the words had been uttered. Ruzena raised her glass and whispered: "Yes, to our child," and downed her brandy in one gulp.

The trumpeter quickly did his best to make her forget this inept toast by changing the subject, asserting yet again that he had been thinking of Ruzena every hour of every day.

She said that in the capital the trumpeter was surely surrounded by women more interesting than she.

He responded that he was fed up with their refinement and pretentiousness. He preferred Ruzena to all other women, regretting only that he lived so far from her. Didn't she want to come to work in the capital?

She replied that she would like to live in the capital. But it was not easy to find a job there.

He smiled condescendingly and said that he had many connections in the hospitals there and could with no difficulty get her a job.

He talked to her this way for a long time, continuing to hold her hand, and thus didn't notice when a girl approached them. Unafraid of intruding, she said enthusiastically: "You're Mister Klima! I recognized you right away! I just want your autograph!"

Klima blushed. He was holding Ruzena's hand and had made a declaration of love to her in a public place in front of everyone present. He thought that it was as if he were in an ancient arena and that the whole world had been transformed into amused spectators observing with malicious laughter his struggle for life.

The girl handed him a piece of paper, and Klima wanted to sign it as quickly as possible, but he had no pen and neither did she.

"Do you have a pen?" he asked Ruzena, whispering because he feared the girl would notice his use of the familiar pronoun. But he instantly realized that the familiar was far less intimate than his hand in Ruzena's, and he repeated his question more loudly: "Do you have a pen?"

Ruzena shook her head, and the girl went back to her table, where several boys and girls instantly took advantage of the opportunity and with the girl rushed over to Klima. They handed him a pen and from a notepad tore sheets of paper for him to sign.

From the standpoint of the plan, this was all to the good. Ruzena would be all the more easily convinced that he loved her if there were numerous witnesses to their intimacy. But however rational he was, anxiety's irrationality threw the trumpeter into a panic. The idea came to him that Ruzena was conniving with all these people. In a confused vision he imagined them all testifying against him in a paternity case: "Yes, we saw them, they were sitting facing each other like lovers, he was caressing her hand and gazing lovingly into her eyes . . ."

The anxiety was further aggravated by the trumpeter's vanity; he actually considered Ruzena not beautiful enough for him to hold her hand in public. That was a bit unjust to Ruzena. She was much prettier than she seemed to him at this moment. Just as love makes the beloved woman more beautiful, anxiety inspired by a woman one fears brings her smallest flaws into disproportionate relief . . .

"I don't like this place," said Klima when they were finally alone again. "Do you want to go for a drive?"

She was eager to see his car, and she agreed. Klima paid the check, and they left the brasserie. Opposite them was a broad, yellow sand path. Some ten men were lined up there, facing the brasserie. For the most part they were old men, wearing red armbands on the sleeves of their wrinkled jackets and holding long poles in their hands.

Klima was dumbfounded: "What is that?"

Ruzena responded: "It's nothing, show me your car," and she quickly started to drag him away.

But Klima was unable to take his eyes off the men. He could not fathom the purpose of the long poles with wire loops at the ends. The men were like lamplighters, like fishermen in search of flying fish, like militiamen with a secret weapon.

While he was scrutinizing them, he thought one of them was smiling at him. He was afraid, even afraid for himself, thinking that he was beginning to hallucinate and seeing everyone as following and watching him. He let Ruzena drag him away to the parking lot.

9

"I'd like to go somewhere far away with you," he said. He had his right arm around Ruzena's shoulders and his left hand on the steering wheel. "Somewhere south. Where you drive for hours on a corniche along the sea. Have you been to Italy?"

"No."

"Well then, promise you'll come with me."

"Aren't you overdoing it a bit?"

Ruzena had said it only out of modesty, but the trumpeter was instantly on guard, as if that "overdoing it" applied to all of his demagogy, which she had suddenly seen through. But he could no longer back out: "Yes, I'm overdoing it. I always have crazy ideas. That's how I am. But unlike other people, I carry out my crazy ideas. Believe me, nothing is more beautiful than to carry out crazy ideas. I'd like my whole life to be one single crazy idea. I'd like us not to go back to the spa, I'd like us to go on driving nonstop until we get to the sea. Down there I'd find a job in a band, and we'd go along the coast from one resort to another."

He stopped the sedan at a spot with a scenic view. They got out, and he suggested they take a walk in the forest. They walked a few minutes and then sat down on a wooden bench dating from the time when people went by car less and appreciated excursions in the forest more. He kept his arm around Ruzena's shoulders and suddenly said in a sad voice: "Everybody imagines

I have a very happy life. That's a big mistake. I'm really very unhappy. Not only these last few months, but for several years now."

If Ruzena regarded the idea of a trip to Italy excessive and thought about it with vague suspicion (very few of their fellow citizens were allowed to travel abroad), the sadness that emanated from these words of Klima's had for her a pleasant odor. She sniffed it as if it were roast pork.

"How can you be unhappy?"

"How I can be unhappy . . ." said the trumpeter with a sigh.

"You're famous, you've got a beautiful car, you've got money, you've got a pretty wife . . ."

"Maybe pretty, yes . . ." the trumpeter said bitterly.

"I know," said Ruzena. "She's not young anymore. She's your age, right?"

The trumpeter saw that Ruzena was probably fully informed on the subject of his wife, and this angered him. But he went on: "Yes, she's my age."

"You're not old. You look like a kid," said Ruzena.

"But a man needs a woman younger than he is," said Klima. "And an artist more than anyone else. I need youth, you can't imagine, Ruzena, how much I appreciate your youth. I sometimes think I can't go on like this. I feel a frantic desire to free myself. To start all over again and in another way. Ruzena, your phone call—suddenly I was sure it was a message sent by fate."

"Really?" she asked softly.

"Why do you think I called you back right away? All at once I felt that I couldn't lose any more time. That I had to see you right now, right now, right now . . ." He fell silent and gazed into her eyes for a long while: "Do you love me?"

"Yes. And you?"

"I love you madly," he said.

"Me too."

He leaned over her and put his mouth against hers. It was a healthy mouth, a young mouth, a pretty mouth with prettily shaped soft lips and carefully brushed teeth, with everything in place, and the fact is that two months earlier he had yielded to the temptation of kissing these lips. But precisely because that mouth had charmed him, he had seen it at the time through a mist of desire and knew nothing of it in reality: the tongue had been like a flame and the saliva had been an intoxicating liqueur. Only now, having lost its charm, was the mouth suddenly what it was, a *real* mouth, an industrious orifice through which the young woman had already taken in cubic meters of dumplings, potatoes, and soups, a mouth containing teeth pocked with fillings and saliva that was no longer an intoxicating liqueur but the cousin of a glob of spit. The tongue in the trumpeter's mouth had the effect of an unappetizing mouthful impossible to swallow and unseemly to remove.

The kiss finally over, they got up and set off again. Ruzena was almost happy, but she was well aware that the reason she had telephoned the trumpeter and had compelled him to come here was oddly being avoided in their conversation. She had no desire to discuss it at length. On the contrary, what they were talking about now seemed more pleasant and more important to her. Yet she wished that this reason, now being passed over in silence, were present, even if only discreetly and modestly. And so when Klima, after various declarations of love, announced that he would do everything he could to live with Ruzena, she pointed out: "You're very sweet, but we have to remember that I'm no longer all alone."

"Yes," said Klima, and he knew that this was the moment he had dreaded from the very first, the weakest link in his demagogy.

"Yes, you're right," he said. "You're not alone. But that's not really the main thing. I want to be with you because I love you, and not because you're pregnant."

"Yes," said Ruzena.

"Nothing's more horrible than a marriage that has no other reason than a child conceived by mistake. And actually, darling, if I may speak frankly, I want you to be the way you were before. There should be just the two of us, and nobody else in between. Do you understand me?"

"Oh no, that's not possible, I can't agree to that, I never could," Ruzena protested.

She said this not because she was convinced of it deep down. The definitive word she had gotten from Dr. Skreta two days earlier was so fresh that she was still disconcerted. She was not following a minutely calculated plan but was completely absorbed by the idea of her pregnancy, which she was experiencing as a great event and still more as a stroke of luck and an opportunity that would not so easily come again. She was like a pawn reaching the end of the chessboard and becoming a queen. She was delighted by the thought of her unexpected, unprecedented power. She saw that at her summons things had been set in motion, the famous trumpeter coming from the capital to see her, to take her for a drive in a magnificent car, to make declarations of love to her. No doubt there was a connection between her pregnancy and that sudden power. If she did not wish to give up her power, she could not give up her pregnancy.

That is why the trumpeter had to go on rolling his heavy stone uphill. "Darling, it's not a family I want, it's love. For me, you are love, and when there's a child, love gives way to family. To boredom. To worries. To monotony. Lover gives way to mother. For me, you're not a mother but a lover, and I don't want to share you with anyone. Even with a child."

These were beautiful words, and Ruzena heard them with pleasure but shook her head: "No, I couldn't. It's just as much your child. I couldn't get rid of your child."

Unable to find new arguments, he kept repeating the same words and dreading that she would finally see through their hypocrisy.

"You're over thirty. Haven't you ever wanted a child?"

True, he had never wanted a child. He loved Kamila too much for her to be hampered by the presence of a child. What he had just asserted to Ruzena was not pure invention. He had in fact been uttering exactly the same words to his wife for years, sincerely, without deceit.

"You've been married six years and don't have a child. It thrills me so to think of giving you a child."

He saw that everything was going against him. The exceptional nature of his love for Kamila convinced Ruzena of his wife's infertility and inspired misplaced audacity in the nurse.

It began to grow chilly, the sun was sinking toward the horizon, time was passing, Klima went on repeating what he had already said, and Ruzena repeated her "No, no, I couldn't." He felt that he was at a dead end; he no longer knew what to do and thought he was going to lose everything. He was so nervous he forgot to hold her hand, forgot to kiss her, forgot to put tenderness into his voice. He realized this with dread and tried hard to pull himself together. He stopped, smiled at her, and took her in his arms. It was a tired embrace of fatigue. He clasped her to him, his head pressed against her face, and it was actually a way of leaning on her, of resting, catching his breath, because it seemed to him that he lacked strength for the long road still ahead.

But Ruzena too had her back against the wall. Like him she had run out of arguments, and she felt you could not go on for long merely repeating "no" to a man you wanted to win.

The embrace lasted a long while, and when Klima let Ruzena slip out of his arms she lowered her head and said in a resigned tone: "All right, tell me what I should do."

Klima could not believe his ears. These were sudden and unexpected words, and they were an immense relief. So immense that he had to make a great effort to control himself and not show it too clearly. He caressed the young woman's cheek and said that Dr. Skreta was a friend of his and all Ruzena had to do was appear before the committee in three days. He would go with her. She had nothing to be afraid of.

Ruzena didn't protest, and he regained the desire to continue playing his role. He put his arm around her shoulders and again and again stopped talking to kiss her (his joy was so great that the kisses were once more obscured by a veil of mist). He repeated that Ruzena should move to the capital. He even repeated his words about a trip to the seashore.

Then the sun disappeared below the horizon, the darkness deepened in the forest, and a round moon appeared above the tops of the fir trees. They went back to the car. As they were reaching the road they found themselves in a beam of light. For a moment they thought it was the headlights of a passing car, but it became instantly obvious that the light was focused on them. The beam was coming from a motorcycle parked on the other side of the road; a man was on it, watching them.

"Hurry up, let's go. Please!" said Ruzena.

When they were near the car, the man on the motorcycle got off and moved toward them. Klima could only make out a dark silhouette because the parked motorcycle was lighting the man from behind, and the trumpeter had the light in his eyes.

"Come here!" the man shouted, rushing toward Ruzena. "I have to talk to you. We've got things to talk about! A lot of things!" His voice was tense and confused.

The trumpeter too was tense and confused, and all he could feel was a kind of irritation at the lack of respect: "The young lady is with me, not with you," he announced.

"You too, I have to talk to you, you know!" the stranger screamed at the trumpeter. "You think because you're famous you can do anything you want! You figure you're going to play games with her! That you can turn her head! It's very easy for you! I could do the same thing if I were you!"

Ruzena took advantage of the motorcyclist's focus on the trumpeter to slip into the car. The motorcyclist leaped toward the door. But the window was closed and the young woman turned on the radio. The car resounded with loud music. Then the trumpeter also slipped into the car and slammed the door. The music was deafening. Through the windshield they could only make out the silhouette of a screaming man and his gesticulating arms.

"He's a madman who's always following me," said Ruzena. "Quick, please let's get going!"

10

He parked the car, took Ruzena to Karl Marx House, gave her a kiss, and when she disappeared behind the door, felt as tired as after four sleepless nights. It was getting late. Klima was hungry and didn't feel even strong enough to take the wheel and drive. He yearned to hear soothing words from Bertlef and walked across the park to the Richmond.

Arriving at the entrance, he was struck by the sight of a large poster lit by a street lamp. His name was on it in big, clumsy letters, and below it, in smaller letters, were the names of Dr. Skreta and the piano-playing pharmacist. The poster had been done by hand and included an amateur drawing of a golden trumpet.

The trumpeter considered it a good omen that Dr. Skreta had arranged the concert promotion so quickly, because such speed seemed to indicate that Skreta was a man he could count on. He went up the stairs in a hurry and knocked at Bertlef's door.

There was no answer.

He knocked again, and again there was no answer.

Before he could think whether he was arriving at the wrong time (the American was known for his many relationships with women) his hand pushed down on the door handle. The door was unlocked. The trumpeter went into the room and stopped. He could see nothing. Nothing but a glow coming from a location on the wall of the room. It was a strange glow; it did not resemble the white light of a fluorescent tube or the yellow one of an electric bulb. It was a bluish light, and it filled the whole room.

Then a belated thought reached his imprudent fingers and suggested to him that he was possibly being indiscreet by intruding, without the slightest invitation, on people at a late hour. Afraid of being rude, he stepped back into the corridor and quickly closed the door.

But he was so confused that instead of leaving he remained standing at the door, striving to understand that strange light. He wondered if the American might be naked in his room and taking a sunbath under an ultraviolet lamp. But then the door opened and Bertlef appeared. He was not naked, he was wearing the same outfit he had worn in the morning. He smiled at the trumpeter: "I am glad you have come by to see me. Come in."

The trumpeter entered with curiosity, but the room was now lit by an ordinary ceiling lamp.

"I'm afraid I've disturbed you," said the trumpeter.

"Not at all!" Bertlef responded, pointing to the window where the trumpeter thought he had seen the source of the blue light. "I was just sitting here thinking. That's all."

"When I came in just before—excuse me for barging in on you like that—I saw an absolutely extraordinary light."

"A light?" said Bertlef, and he laughed. "You should

not take that pregnancy with such seriousness. It is giving you hallucinations."

"Or else maybe it was because I was coming from the very dark corridor."

"That could be," said Bertlef. "But tell me how things turned out!"

The trumpeter began his story, and after a while Bertlef interrupted: "Are you hungry?"

The trumpeter nodded, and Bertlef took a package of crackers and a can of ham out of a cupboard and immediately opened them.

Klima went on talking, greedily downing his dinner and looking inquiringly at Bertlef.

"I believe everything will turn out well," Bertlef comforted him.

"And what do you think about the fellow who was waiting for us by the car?"

Bertlef shrugged: "I don't know. Anyway, it's no longer important."

"That's right. I have to think instead about how to explain to Kamila why that conference took so long."

It was already very late. Comforted and reassured, the trumpeter got into his car and set off for the capital. He was accompanied all the way by an enormous round moon.

Third Day

1

It is Wednesday morning, and the spa is once again awake for an active day. Torrents of water are flowing into tubs, masseurs are kneading naked backs, and a private car has just pulled into the parking lot. Not the big, luxurious white sedan that had been in the same spot the day before, but the ordinary car one can see so many of in this country. The man behind the wheel is about forty-five, and he is alone. The back seat is cluttered with suitcases.

The man gets out, locks the doors, gives a five-crown coin to the parking-lot attendant, and heads toward Karl Marx House; he walks along the corridor until he comes to the door with Dr. Skreta's name on it. He enters the waiting room and knocks on the office door. A nurse appears, the man introduces himself, and then Dr. Skreta comes out to greet him: "Jakub! When did you get here?"

"Just now!"

"Wonderful! We've got a lot of things to discuss. Listen . . ." he says after a moment's thought, "I can't leave right now. Come with me into the examining room. I'll lend you a coat."

Jakub was not a physician and had never before

entered a gynecologist's examining room. But Dr. Skreta had already taken him by the arm and led him into a white room, where an undressed woman was lying on an examination table with her legs spread.

"Give the doctor a coat," Skreta said to the nurse, who opened a cabinet and handed Jakub a white coat. "Come take a look, I want you to confirm my diagnosis," he said to Jakub, inviting him to go near the patient, who was visibly quite pleased by the idea that the mystery of her ovaries, which despite great efforts had not yet produced any descendants, was going to be explored by two medical specialists.

Dr. Skreta resumed palpating the patient's womb, uttered some Latin words to which Jakub grunted approval, and then asked: "How long are you staying here?"

"One day."

"One day? That's absurdly brief, we won't be able to discuss anything!"

"It hurts when you touch me like that," said the woman with the raised legs.

"It should hurt a little bit, it's nothing," said Jakub to amuse his friend.

"Yes, the doctor's right," said Skreta. "It's nothing, it's normal. I'm going to prescribe a series of shots for you. Be here every morning at six, and the nurse will give you your shot. You can get dressed now."

"I really came to say goodbye to you," said Jakub.

"What do you mean, goodbye?"

"I'm going abroad. I've got permission to emigrate."

The woman dressed and took leave of Dr. Skreta and his colleague.

"What a surprise! I never expected that!" Dr. Skreta marveled. "Seeing that you came to say goodbye to me, I'm going to send these women home."

"Doctor," the nurse interrupted, "you sent them away yesterday too. We'll have a big backlog at the end of the week!"

"All right then, send in the next one," said Dr. Skreta with a sigh.

The nurse sent in the next one, whom the two men glanced at absentmindedly, noting that she was prettier than the last one.

Dr. Skreta asked her how she had been feeling since she began the baths, and then asked her to undress.

"It took forever to get my passport. But after that I was ready to leave in two days. I didn't want to say goodbye to anyone."

"Then I'm all the happier that you stopped here," said Dr. Skreta, and then he asked the young woman to climb up on the examination table. He put on a rubber glove and thrust his hand into the patient.

"I don't want to see anybody but you and Olga," said Jakub. "I hope she's all right."

"Everything's fine, fine," said Skreta, but from the sound of his voice it was obvious he was not aware of what he was saying to Jakub. He was concentrating all his attention on the patient: "We're going to do a little procedure," he said. "Don't worry, you won't feel a thing." Then he opened the glass door of a cabinet and took out a hypodermic syringe with a small plastic nozzle at the end instead of a needle.

"What's that?" asked Jakub.

"During many years of practicing medicine, I've perfected some extremely effective new methods. You might find it selfish of me, but for the moment I consider them my secret."

Her voice more flirtatious than fearful, the woman lying with her legs spread asked: "It won't hurt?"

"Not at all," replied Dr. Skreta, dipping the syringe into a test tube he was handling with meticulous care. Then he came close to the woman, inserted the syringe between her legs, and pushed the plunger.

"Did that hurt?"

"No," said the patient.

"I also came here to give you back the tablet."

Dr. Skreta barely took notice of Jakub's words. He was still busy with his patient. He inspected her from head to toe with a serious and thoughtful expression and said: "In your case, it would really be a shame if you didn't have a child. You've got long legs, a well-developed pelvis, a beautiful rib cage, and quite a pleasant face."

He touched the patient's face, chucked her chin, and said: "A nice jaw, sturdy and well-shaped."

Then he took hold of her thigh: "And you've got marvelously firm bones. It looks like they're shining under your muscles."

He went on for a time praising the patient while manipulating her body, and she didn't protest or giggle any longer, for the seriousness of the physician's interest in her put his touchings well on this side of shamelessness.

At last he indicated that she should get dressed, and he turned to his friend: "What were you saying?"

"That I came to give you back the tablet."

"What tablet?"

As she was dressing the woman said: "Well, Doctor, do you think there's any hope for me?"

"I'm extremely satisfied," said Dr. Skreta. "I think that things are developing positively and that we, you and I both, can count on a success."

Thanking him, the woman left the examining room, and then Jakub said: "Years ago you gave me a tablet nobody else would give me. Now that I'm leaving, I think I won't need it anymore, and I should give it back to you."

"Keep it! The tablet could be just as useful elsewhere as it is here."

"No, no. The tablet was part of this country. I want to leave in this country everything that belongs to it," said Jakub.

"Doctor, I'm going to bring in the next one," said the nurse.

"Send all those females home," said Dr. Skreta. "I've done my work for today. You'll see, that last one will surely have a child. That's enough for a day, no?"

The nurse looked at the doctor tenderly and yet showed not the slightest intention of obeying him.

Dr. Skreta understood this look: "All right, don't

send them away; just tell them I'll be back in half an hour."

"Doctor, you said half an hour yesterday too, and I had to run after you in the street."

"Don't worry, my dear, I'll be back in half an hour," said Skreta, and he motioned his friend to return the white coat to the nurse. Then they left the building and went straight across the park to the Richmond.

2

They went up to the second floor and followed the long red carpet to the end of the corridor. Dr. Skreta opened a door and with his friend entered a cramped but pleasant room.

"It's nice of you," said Jakub, "always to have a room for me here."

"I've got some rooms set aside now at this end of the corridor for my special patients. Next to your room is a beautiful corner suite where cabinet ministers and industrialists stayed in the old days. I've put up my prize patient there, a rich American whose family originated here. He's become something of a friend."

"And where does Olga live?"

"In Marx House, like me. Don't worry, she's all right there."

"The main thing is that you're looking after her. How is she doing?"

"She has the usual problems of women with fragile nerves."

"I told you in my letter about the life she's had."

"Most women come here to gain fertility. In your ward's case, it would be better if she didn't take advantage of her fertility. Have you ever seen her naked?"

"My God! Certainly not!" said Jakub.

"Well, take a look at her! She has tiny breasts hanging from her chest like two little plums. You can see her ribs. From now on look more closely at rib cages. A real thorax should be aggressive, outgoing, it has to expand as if it wants to take up as much space as possible. On the other hand, there are rib cages that are on the defensive, that retreat from the outside world; it's like a straitjacket getting tighter and tighter around someone and finally suffocating him. That's the case with hers. Tell her to show it to you."

"It's the last thing I'd do," said Jakub.

"You're afraid that if you saw it you'd no longer regard her as your ward."

"On the contrary," said Jakub. "I'm afraid of feeling even more sorry for her."

"Incidentally, old friend," said Skreta, "that American is really an extremely odd type."

"Where can I see her right now?" asked Jakub.

"Who?"

"Olga."

"You can't see her now. She's having her treatment.

She has to spend the whole morning in the pool."

"I don't want to miss her. Can I phone her?"

Dr. Skreta lifted the receiver and dialed a number without interrupting his conversation with his friend: "I'm going to introduce you, and I want you to study him thoroughly for me. You're psychologically astute. You're going to see right through him. I've got plans for him."

"Like what?" asked Jakub, but Dr. Skreta was already talking into the receiver: "Is this Ruzena? How are you? . . . . Don't worry, nausea is normal in your condition. I wanted to ask you if a patient of mine is in the pool right now, your neighbor in the room next door. . . . Yes? Good, tell her she's got a visitor from the capital, above all tell her not to go anywhere. . . . Yes, he'll be waiting for her at noon in front of the thermal building."

Skreta hung up. "Well, you heard that. You're going to see her again at noon. Damn, what were we just talking about?"

"About the American."

"Yes," said Skreta. "He's an extremely odd type. I cured his wife. They'd been unable to have children."

"And what's he here for?"

"His heart."

"You said you've got plans for him."

"It's humiliating," said Skreta indignantly, "what a physician is forced to do in this country in order to make a decent living! Klima, the famous trumpeter, is coming here. I have to accompany him on the drums!"

Jakub didn't think Skreta was being serious, but he pretended to be surprised: "What, you play the drums?"

"Yes, my friend! What can I do, now that I'm going to have a family?"

"What?" Jakub exclaimed, this time truly surprised. "A family? Are you telling me you're married?"

"Yes," said Skreta.

"To Suzy?"

Suzy was a doctor at the spa who had been Skreta's girlfriend for years, but at the last moment he had always succeeded in avoiding marriage.

"Yes, to Suzy," said Skreta. "You know that every Sunday I used to climb up to the scenic view with her."

"So you're really married," said Jakub with melancholy.

"Every time we climbed up there," Skreta went on, "Suzy tried to convince me we should get married. And I'd be so worn out by the climb that I felt old and that there was nothing left for me but to marry. But in the end I always controlled myself, and when we came back down from the scenic view my strength would come back and I'd no longer want to get married. But one day Suzy made us take a detour, and the climb took so long I agreed to get married even before we got to the top. And now we're expecting a child, and I have to think a bit about money. The American also paints religious pictures. One could make a lot of money from that. What do you think?"

"Do you believe there's a market for religious pictures?"

"A fantastic market! All it takes, old friend, is to put up a stand next to the church on pilgrimage days and, at a hundred crowns apiece, we'd make a fortune! I could sell them for him and we'd split fifty-fifty."

"And what does he say?"

"The fellow has so much money he doesn't know what to do with it, and I'm sure I wouldn't be able to get him to go into business with me," said Skreta with a curse.

3

Olga clearly saw Nurse Ruzena waving to her from the edge of the pool, but she went on swimming and pretended she had not seen her.

The two women didn't like each other. Dr. Skreta had put Olga in a small room next to Ruzena's. Ruzena was in the habit of playing the radio very loud, and Olga liked quiet. She had rapped on the wall at various times, and the nurse's only response was to turn up the volume.

Ruzena persisted in waving and finally succeeded in telling the patient that a visitor from the capital would be meeting her at noon.

Olga realized that it was Jakub, and she felt immense joy. And instantly she was surprised by this joy: How can I be feeling such pleasure at the idea of seeing him again?

Olga was actually one of those modern women who readily divide themselves into a person who lives life and a person who observes it.

But even the Olga who observed life was rejoicing. For she understood very well that it was utterly excessive for Olga (the one who lived life) to rejoice so impetuously, and because she (the one who observed life) was mischievous this excessiveness gave her pleasure. She smiled at the idea that Jakub would be frightened if he knew of the fierceness of her joy.

The hands of the clock above the pool showed a quarter to twelve. Olga wondered how Jakub would react if she were to throw her arms around his neck and kiss him passionately. She swam to the edge of the pool, climbed out, and went to a cubicle to change. She regretted a little not having been informed of Jakub's visit earlier in the day. She would have been better dressed. Now she was wearing an uninteresting little gray suit that spoiled her good mood.

There were times, such as a few minutes earlier while swimming in the pool, when she totally forgot her appearance. But now she was planted in front of the cubicle's small mirror and seeing herself in a gray suit. A few minutes earlier she had smiled mischievously at the idea that she could throw her arms around Jakub's neck and kiss him passionately. But she had that idea in the pool, where she had been swimming bodilessly, like a disembodied thought. Now that she had suddenly been provided with a body and a suit, she was far away from that joyous fantasy, and she knew that she was exactly what to her great anger Jakub always saw her as: a touching little girl who needed help.

If Olga had been a little more foolish, she would have found herself quite pretty. But since she was an intelligent girl, she considered herself much uglier than she really was, for she was actually neither ugly nor pretty, and any man with normal aesthetic requirements would gladly spend the night with her.

But since Olga delighted in dividing herself in two, the one who observed life now interrupted the one who lived life: What did it matter that she was like this or like that? Why suffer over a reflection in a mirror? Wasn't she something other than an object for men's eyes? Other than merchandise putting herself on the market? Was she incapable of being independent of her appearance, at the very least to the degree that any man can be?

She left the thermal building and saw a good-natured and touching face. She knew that instead of extending his hand to her he was going to pat her on the head like a good little girl. Sure enough, that is what he did.

"Where are we having lunch?" he asked.

She suggested the patients' dining room, where there was a vacant place at her table.

The patients' dining room was immense, filled with tables and people squeezed closely together having lunch. Jakub and Olga sat down and then waited a long time before a waitress served them soup. Two other people were sitting at their table, and they tried to engage in conversation with Jakub, whom they immediately classified as a member of the sociable family of patients. It was therefore only in snatches during the general talk at the table that Jakub could question Olga about a few practical details: Was she satisfied with the food here, was she satisfied with the doctor, was she satisfied with the treatment? When he asked about her lodgings, she answered that she had a dreadful neighbor. She motioned with her head to a nearby table, where Ruzena was having lunch.

Their table companions took their leave, and looking at Ruzena, Jakub said: "Hegel has a curious reflection on the Grecian profile, whose beauty, according to him, comes from the fact that the nose and the brow form a single line that highlights the upper part of the head, the seat of intelligence and of the mind. Looking at your neighbor, I notice that her whole face, on the other hand, is concentrated on the mouth. Look how intensely she chews, and how she's talking loudly at the same time. Hegel would be disgusted by such importance being attached to the lower part, the animal part, of the face, and yet this girl I dislike is quite pretty."

"Do you think so?" asked Olga, her voice betraying annoyance.

That is why Jakub hastened to say: "At any rate I'd be afraid of being ground up into tiny bits by that ruminant's mouth." And he added: "Hegel would be more satisfied with you. The dominant part of your face is the brow, which instantly tells everyone about your intelligence."

"Logic like that infuriates me," said Olga sharply. "It tries to show that a human being's physiognomy is imprinted on his soul. It's absolute nonsense. I picture my soul with a strong chin and sensual lips, but my chin is small and so is my mouth. If I'd never seen myself in a mirror and had to describe my outside appearance from what I know of the inside of me, the portrait wouldn't look at all like me! I am not at all the person I look like!"

4

It is difficult to find a word to characterize Jakub's relation to Olga. She was the daughter of a friend of his who had been executed when Olga was seven years old. Jakub decided at that time to take the little orphan under his wing. He had no children, and such obligation-free fatherhood appealed to him. He playfully called Olga his ward.

They were now in Olga's room. She plugged in a hotplate and put a small saucepan of water on it, and Jakub realized that he could not bring himself to reveal the purpose of his visit to her. He didn't dare tell her that he had come to say goodbye, was afraid the news would take on too pathetic a dimension and generate an emotional climate between them that he regarded as uncalled for. He had long suspected her of being secretly in love with him.

Olga took two cups out of the cupboard, spooned instant coffee into them, and poured boiling water. Jakub stirred in a sugar cube and heard Olga say: "Please tell me, Jakub, what kind of man was my father really?"

"Why do you ask?"

"Did he really have nothing to blame himself for?"

"What are you thinking of?" asked Jakub, amazed. Olga's father had been officially rehabilitated sometime earlier, and this political figure who had been sentenced to death and executed had been publicly proclaimed innocent. No one doubted his innocence.

"That's not what I mean," said Olga. "I mean just the opposite."

"I don't understand," said Jakub.

"I was wondering if he hadn't done to others exactly what was done to him. There wasn't a grain of difference between him and those who sent him to the gallows. They had the same beliefs, they were the same fanatics. They were convinced that even the slightest differences could put the revolution in mortal danger, and they suspected everyone. They sent him to his death in the name of holy things he himself believed in. Why then couldn't he have behaved toward others the same way they behaved toward him?"

"Time flies terribly fast, and the past is becoming

more and more incomprehensible," said Jakub after a moment's hesitation. "What do you know of your father besides a few letters, a few pages of his diary they kindly returned to you, and a few recollections from his friends?"

But Olga insisted: "Why are you so evasive? I asked you a perfectly clear question. Was my father like the ones who sent him to his death?"

"It's possible," said Jakub with a shrug.

"Then why couldn't he too have been capable of committing the same cruelties?"

"Theoretically," replied Jakub very slowly, "theoretically he was capable of doing to others exactly the same thing they did to him. There isn't a man in this world who isn't capable, with a relatively light heart, of sending a fellow human to his death. At any rate I've never met one. If men one day come to change in this regard, they'll lose a basic human attribute. They'll no longer be men but creatures of another species."

"You people are wonderful!" Olga exclaimed as if shouting at thousands of Jakubs. "When you turn everybody into murderers your own murders stop being crimes and just become an inevitable human attribute."

"Most people move around inside an idyllic circle between their home and their work," said Jakub. "They live in a secure territory beyond good and evil. They're sincerely appalled by the sight of a murderer. But taking them out of this secure territory is enough to make them murderers themselves, without their knowing how it happened. There are tests and temptations that only rarely turn up during the course of history. Nobody can resist them. But it's utterly useless to talk about this. What counts for you isn't what your father was theoretically capable of doing, because there's no way of proving it anyway. The only thing that should interest you is what he actually did or didn't do. And in that sense he had a clear conscience."

"Are you absolutely sure?"

"Absolutely. No one knew him better than I did."

"I'm really glad to hear this from you," said Olga. "Because I didn't ask you the question by chance. For a while now I've been getting anonymous letters. They say I'm wrong to play the daughter of a martyr, because my father, before he was executed, himself sent to prison innocent people whose only offense was to have an idea of the world different from his."

"Nonsense," said Jakub.

"These letters describe him as a relentless fanatic and cruel man. Of course they're spiteful anonymous letters, but they're not the letters of a primitive. They're not exaggerated, they're concrete and precise, and I almost ended up believing them."

"It's always the same kind of revenge," said Jakub. "I'm going to tell you something. When they arrested your father, the prisons were full of people the revolution had sent there in the first wave of terror. The prisoners recognized him as a well-known Communist, and at the first chance they pounced on him and beat him unconscious. The guards watched, smiling sadistically."

"I know," said Olga, and Jakub realized he had told her a story she had heard many times. He had long ago resolved never again to talk about these things, but without success. People who have been in an automobile accident cannot help remembering it.

"I know," Olga repeated, "but it doesn't surprise me. The prisoners were jailed without a trial, very often without any grounds. And all of a sudden they were face to face with one of the men they considered responsible!"

"From the moment your father put on the prison uniform, he was a prisoner among prisoners. There was no sense in harming him, especially under the guards' complacent eyes. It was nothing but cowardly revenge. The vilest desire to trample on a defenseless victim. And these letters you got are fruits of the same kind of revenge, which I now see is stronger than time itself."

"But Jakub! Nevertheless a hundred thousand people were put in prison! And thousands never came back! And not a single one of those responsible was ever punished! This desire for revenge is really just an unsatisfied desire for justice!"

"Taking revenge on the father through the daughter has nothing to do with justice. Remember that because of your father you lost your home, you were forced out of your home town, you were denied the right to attend the university. Because of a dead father you barely knew! And because of your father should you be persecuted now? I'm going to tell you the saddest discovery

of my life: the persecuted are no better than the persecutors. I can easily imagine the roles reversed. You
might see in this logic the desire to shift your father's
responsibility onto the Creator who made man as he is.
And maybe it's good for you to see things this way.
Because to come to the conclusion that there's no difference between the guilty and the victims is to *abandon all hope*. And that, my girl, is what is called *hell*."

5

Ruzena's two colleagues were burning with impatience. They wanted to know how the previous day's
meeting with Klima had gone, but they were on duty
at the other end of the thermal building, and it was
not until about three o'clock that they could get to
their friend and bombard her with questions.

Ruzena hesitated to answer and finally said uncer-
tainly: "He said he loved me and he'd marry me."

"You see! I told you so!" said the thin one. "And is he
going to get a divorce?"

"He said yes."

"He'll have to," the fortyish one said cheerfully. "A
baby's a baby. And his wife's never had one."

Now Ruzena had to admit the truth: "He said he's
going to take me to Prague. He's going to find me a

job there. He said we're going to Italy on vacation. But he doesn't want a child right away. And he's right. The first years are the most beautiful, and if we had a child we wouldn't be able to make the most of each other."

The fortyish one was stunned: "What, you're going to have an abortion?"

Ruzena nodded.

"You've gone crazy!" the thin one exclaimed.

"He's twisted you around his little finger," said the fortyish one. "The minute you get rid of the child, he'll send you packing!"

"Why would he?"

"You want to bet?"

"Even if he loves me?"

"And how do you know he loves you?" said the fortyish one.

"He told me he does!"

"And why didn't you hear from him for two months?"

"He was afraid of love," said Ruzena.

"What?"

"How can I explain it to you? He was afraid of being in love with me."

"And that's why he gave no sign of life?"

"It was a test he set himself. He wanted to be sure he couldn't forget me. That's understandable, isn't it?"

"I see," said the fortyish one. "And when he found out he'd knocked you up, he suddenly realized he couldn't forget you."

"He said he's glad I'm pregnant. Not because of the child, but because I phoned him. It made him realize he loved me."

"My God, what an idiot you are!" the thin one exclaimed.

"I don't see why I'm an idiot."

"Because this child is the only thing you've got," said the fortyish one. "If you give up the child, you'll have nothing, and he'll spit on you."

"I want him to want me for my own sake and not for the child's sake!"

"Who do you think you are? Why would he want you for your own sake?"

They discussed the matter passionately for a long time. Her two colleagues went on repeating to Ruzena that the child was her only trump card and that she must not give it up.

"I'd never have an abortion, I can tell you that. Never, do you understand? Never," the thin one declared.

Ruzena suddenly felt like a little girl and said (they were the same words that, the day before, had restored Klima's desire to live): "So tell me what I should do!"

"Don't give in," said the fortyish one, and then she opened a drawer and took out a tube of tablets. "Here, take one! You're a nervous wreck. It'll calm you down."

Ruzena put the tablet in her mouth and swallowed it.

"Keep the tube. Three times a day, but take them only when you need to calm down. So you don't go doing stupid things while you're agitated. Don't forget he's a slippery character. It's not his first time! But this time he won't get out of it so easily!"

Once more she didn't know what to do. A little while ago she had thought her mind was made up, but her colleagues' arguments seemed convincing, and once more she was upset. Torn by indecision, she went downstairs.

In the building's entrance hall, an excited, red-faced young man rushed toward her.

"I told you never to wait for me here," she said, looking at him rancorously. "And after what happened yesterday, I can't believe you've got the gall!"

"Please don't be angry!" the young man cried out in a tone of desperation.

"Shush!" she yelled. "And on top of it don't make a scene here too," and she turned to go.

"Don't go away like that if you don't want me to make a scene!"

There was nothing she could do. Patients were coming and going through the building lobby and staff people in white coats passing by. She didn't want to attract attention, and so she had to stay and try hard to look natural: "All right, what do you want?" she said in an undertone.

"Nothing. I only wanted you to forgive me. I'm really sorry about what I did. But please swear to me there's nothing between you and him."

"I already told you there's nothing between us."

"Then swear!"

"Don't be a child. I don't swear to stupid things like that."

"Because something's happened between you."

"I already said no. And if you don't believe me, we've got nothing more to talk about. He's just a friend. Don't I have the right to have friends? I respect him, I'm glad he's my friend."

"I understand. I don't blame you," said the young man.

"He's giving a concert here tomorrow. I hope you're not going to spy on me."

"I won't if you give me your word of honor there's nothing between you."

"I already told you I won't lower myself by giving my word of honor for things like that. But I give you my word of honor that if you spy on me once more, you'll never see me again as long as you live."

"Ruzena, it's because I love you," said the young man unhappily.

"Me too," Ruzena said curtly. "But I don't go making scenes on the highway for your sake."

"That's because you don't love me. You're ashamed of me."

"Don't talk nonsense!"

"You never want to go out with me, to be seen with me . . ."

"Shush!" she repeated, since he had raised his voice. "My father would kill me. I already told you he keeps an eye on me. But now don't be angry, I really have to go."

The young man grabbed her arm: "Don't go yet."

Ruzena raised her eyes to the ceiling in desperation.

The young man said: "If we got married, everything would be different. Then he couldn't say anything. We'd have a child."

"I don't want to have a child," Ruzena said sharply. "I'd rather kill myself than have a child!"

"Why?"

"Because. I don't want a child."

"I love you, Ruzena," the young man said again.

And Ruzena responded: "And that's why you want to drive me to suicide, right?"

"Suicide?" he asked, surprised.

"Yes! Suicide!"

"Ruzena!" said the young man.

"You're going to drive me to it, all right! I guarantee you! You're definitely going to drive me to it!"

"Can I come see you this evening?" he asked humbly.

"No, not this evening," said Ruzena. Then, realizing she had to calm him, she added in a more conciliatory tone: "You can phone me here, Frantisek. But not before Monday." She turned to go.

"Wait," said the young man. "I brought you something. So that you'll forgive me," and he offered her a small package.

She took it and quickly went out into the street.

6

"Is Doctor Skreta really such an oddball or is he pretending?" Olga asked Jakub.

"I've been asking myself that ever since I've known him," answered Jakub.

"Oddballs have an easy life when they succeed in making people respect their oddballness," said Olga. "Doctor Skreta is incredibly absentminded. In the middle of a conversation he forgets what he was talking about. Sometimes he starts chatting in the street with somebody and gets to his office two hours late. But nobody dares hold it against him because the doctor is an officially recognized oddball and only a boor would contest his right to oddballness."

"Oddball or not, I believe he looks after you rather well."

"He probably does, but everyone here has the impression that for him the medical practice is something secondary that prevents him from devoting himself to lots of much more important projects. For example, tomorrow he's going to play the drums!"

"Wait a minute," interrupted Jakub. "Is that really so?"

"Of course! The whole spa is covered with posters announcing that the famous trumpeter Klima is giving a concert here tomorrow and that Doctor Skreta will be playing the drums."

"That's incredible," said Jakub. "It's not that I'm at

all surprised to hear that Skreta intends to play the drums. Skreta is the biggest dreamer I've ever known. But I haven't seen him yet realize a single one of his dreams. When we got to know each other, at the university, Skreta didn't have much money. He was always broke and always contriving moneymaking schemes. He had a plan at the time to get a female Welsh terrier, because someone told him puppies of this breed brought four thousand crowns apiece. He quickly figured it out. The bitch would have two litters a year, five puppies each. Two times five makes ten, ten times four thousand makes forty thousand crowns per year. He thought of everything. With a lot of difficulty he got the help of the university dining-hall manager, who promised to let the dog have the daily leftovers. He wrote term papers for two women students who promised to walk the dog every day. His student dormitory didn't allow dogs. So each week he brought the housemother a bouquet of roses until she promised to make an exception for him. He spent two months preparing the ground for his bitch, but we all knew he'd never get her. He needed four thousand crowns to buy her, and no one wanted to lend it to him. No one took him seriously. Everyone considered him a dreamer, surely an exceptionally canny and enterprising one, but only in the realm of the imaginary."

"That's quite charming, but I still don't understand your strange affection for him. He's not reliable. He's incapable of being on time, and he forgets the day after what he promised the day before."

"That's not quite right. He helped me a great deal once. In fact, no one's ever helped me as much."

Jakub thrust his hand into the breast pocket of his jacket and took out a folded piece of tissue paper. He unfolded it to reveal a pale-blue tablet.

"What is it?" asked Olga.

"Poison."

Jakub savored the young woman's inquiring silence for a moment and then went on: "I've had this tablet for more than fifteen years. After my year in prison, there was one thing I understood. You need to have at least one certainty: to remain in control of your own death and of the ability to choose its time and manner. With that certainty, you can put up with a lot of things. You know you can get away from people whenever you want."

"Did you have this tablet with you in prison?"

"Unfortunately not! But I got it as soon as I was released."

"When you didn't need it anymore?"

"In this country you never know when you're going to need a thing like that. And then, for me it was a matter of principle. Every person should be given a poison tablet on the day he reaches maturity. A solemn ceremony should take place on that occasion. Not to prompt him to suicide, but, on the contrary, to allow him to live more securely and serenely. To live knowing he's in control of his own life and his own death."

"And how did you get this poison?"

"Skreta started out as a biochemist in a lab. At first I

asked someone else, but she considered it her moral duty to deny me the poison. Skreta himself compounded the tablet without a moment's hesitation."

"Maybe because he's an oddball."

"Maybe. But mostly because he understood me. He knew that I wasn't a hysteric who liked to play suicide games. He understood what was at stake for me. I'm going to give him back the tablet today. I don't need it anymore."

"So all the dangers are gone?"

"Tomorrow morning I'm leaving the country for good. I've been invited to teach at a university, and I've got permission from the authorities to leave."

He had finally said it. Jakub looked at Olga and saw that she was smiling. She took his hand: "Really? That's very good news! I'm very pleased for you!"

She was showing the same disinterested pleasure he himself would feel if he were to learn that Olga was leaving for a foreign country where she would have a more pleasant life. This was surprising, because he had always feared she had an emotional attachment to him. He was happy that it wasn't so, but he also surprised himself by being a bit upset.

Olga was so interested in Jakub's disclosure that she forgot to go on questioning him about the pale-blue tablet lying between them on the piece of tissue paper, and Jakub had to tell her in detail all the circumstances of his future career.

"I'm extremely pleased you managed it. Here you'd always be suspect. They haven't even let you practice your profession. And what's more, they spend their time preaching love of country. How can you love a country where you're forbidden to work? I can tell you I don't feel any love for my homeland. Is that bad of me?"

"I don't know," said Jakub. "I really don't. As far as I'm concerned, I've been rather attached to this country."

"Maybe it's bad of me," Olga went on, "but I don't feel tied to anything. What could I be attached to here?"

"Even painful memories are ties that bind."

"Bind us to what? To staying in the country where we were born? I don't understand how people can talk about freedom and not get that millstone off their necks. As if a tree were at home where it can't grow. A tree is at home wherever water percolates through the soil."

"And you, do you find enough water here?"

"All in all, yes. Now that they're finally letting me study, I've got what I want. I'm going to do my biology, and I don't want to hear about anything else. I wasn't the one who set up this regime, and I'm not responsible for any of it. But when exactly are you leaving?"

"Tomorrow."

"So soon?" She took his hand. "Since you were nice enough to come and say goodbye to me, please don't be in such a hurry to go."

It continued to be different from what he had expected. She was behaving neither like a young woman secretly in love with him nor like an adopted daughter feeling unfleshly filial love for him. She held his hand with eloquent tenderness, looked him in the eye, and repeated: "Don't be in such a hurry! It makes no sense to me that you're not staying here awhile to say goodbye to me."

Jakub was somewhat perplexed by this: "We'll see," he said. "Skreta's also trying to convince me to stay a little longer."

"You should certainly stay longer," said Olga. "In any case, we have so little time for each other. Now I have to go back to the baths . . ." After a moment's thought she announced that she would not go anywhere while Jakub was here.

"No, no, you should go. You shouldn't miss your treatment. I'll go with you."

"Really?" asked Olga happily. She opened the wardrobe and started to look for something.

The pale-blue tablet was still lying on the unfolded piece of paper on the table, and Olga, the only person in the world to whom Jakub had revealed its existence, was leaning into the wardrobe with her back to the poison. Jakub thought that this pale-blue tablet was the drama of his life, a neglected, nearly forgotten, and probably uninteresting drama. And he told himself that it was high time to rid himself of this uninteresting drama, to say goodbye to it quickly and leave it behind him. He wrapped the tablet in the piece of paper and stuck it into the breast pocket of his jacket.

Olga took a bag out of the wardrobe, put a towel

into it, closed the wardrobe door, and said to Jakub: "I'm ready."

7

Ruzena had been sitting on a park bench for God knows how long, probably unable to budge because her thoughts too were motionless, fixed on a single point.

Yesterday she had still believed what the trumpeter told her. Not only because it was pleasant but also because it was more simple: it provided her a way to give up, with a clear conscience, a fight for which she lacked the strength. But after her colleagues laughed at her, she again mistrusted him and thought of him with hatred, fearing deep down that she was neither cunning nor stubborn enough to win him.

Apathetically she tore open the package Francisck had given her. Inside was something made of pale-blue fabric, and Ruzena realized he had made her a present of a nightgown; a nightgown he wished to see her in every day; every day, a great many days, for the rest of his life. She gazed at the pale-blue fabric and thought she saw that patch of blue run and expand, turn into a pond, a pond of goodness and devotion, a pond of abject love which would end up engulfing her.

Whom did she hate more? The one who did not want her or the one who did?

So she sat rooted to the bench by these two hatreds, oblivious to what was going on around her. A minibus pulled up at the edge of the park, followed by a small green truck from which Ruzena heard dogs howling and barking. The minibus doors opened and out came an old man wearing a red armband on his sleeve. Ruzena was looking straight ahead in a daze, and it was a moment before she was aware of what she was looking at.

The old gentleman shouted an order at the minibus and another old man got out, he too wearing a red armband but also holding a three-meter pole with a wire loop attached to the end. More men got out and lined up in front of the minibus. They were all old men, all with red armbands and holding long poles equipped with wire loops at the tips.

The first man to get out had no pole and gave orders; the old gentlemen, like a squad of bizarre lancers, came to attention and then to at ease a few times. Then the man shouted another order, and the squad of old men headed into the park at a run. There they broke ranks, each one running in a different direction, some along the paths, others on the grass. The patients strolling in the park, the children playing, everyone abruptly stopped to look in amazement at the old gentlemen, armed with long poles, launching an attack.

Ruzena too came out of her meditative stupor to watch what was happening. She recognized her father among the old gentlemen and watched him with dis-gust but without surprise.

A mutt was scampering on the grass around a birch tree. One of the old gentlemen started to run toward it, and the dog looked at him with surprise. The old man brandished the pole, trying to get the wire loop in front of the dog's head. But the pole was long, the old hands were feeble, and the old man missed his objective. The wire loop wavered around the dog's head while the dog watched curiously.

But another pensioner, one with stronger arms, was already rushing to the old man's aid, and the little dog finally found himself prisoner in the wire loop. The old man pulled on the pole, the wire loop dug into the furry neck, and the dog let out a howl. The two pensioners laughed loudly as they dragged the dog along the lawn toward the parked vehicles. They opened the truck's large door, from which a wave of barking rang out; then they threw the mutt in.

For Ruzena what she was seeing was merely a component of her own story: she was an unhappy woman caught between two worlds: Klima's world rejected her, and Frantisek's world, from which she wanted to escape (the world of banality and boredom, the world of failure and capitulation), had come to look for her here in the guise of this assault team as if it were trying to drag her away by a wire loop.

On a sand path a small boy of about ten was desperately calling his dog, which had strayed into the bushes. Running over to the boy came not the dog but

Ruzena's father, armed with a pole. The boy instantly fell silent. He was afraid to call his dog, knowing that the old man was going to take him away. He rushed down the path to escape him, but the old man too started to run. Now they were running side by side, Ruzena's father armed with his pole and the small boy sobbing as he ran. And then the boy turned around and, still running, retraced his steps. Ruzena's father followed suit. Again they were running side by side.

A dachshund came out of the bushes. Ruzena's father extended his pole toward him, but the dog alertly evaded it and ran over to the boy, who lifted him up and hugged him. Other old men rushed over to help Ruzena's father and tear the dachshund out of the boy's arms. The boy was crying, shouting, and grappling with them so that the old men had to twist his arms and put a hand over his mouth because his cries were attracting too much attention from the passersby, who were turning to look but not daring to intervene.

Ruzena didn't want to see any more of her father and his companions. But where to go? Into her little room, where there was a detective novel that she had not finished and that didn't interest her; to the movies, where there was a film she had already seen; to the lobby of the Richmond, where there was a television set on all the time? She opted for television. She got up from her bench, and amid the clamor of the old men, which was continuing from all sides, she was again intensely conscious of what she had in her womb, and she told herself that it was something sacred. It transformed and ennobled her. It distinguished her from these fanatics who were chasing dogs. She told herself that she did not have the right to give up, did not have the right to capitulate, because in her belly she was carrying her only hope; her only admission ticket to the future.

When she reached the edge of the park, she caught sight of Jakub. He was standing on the sidewalk in front of the Richmond, watching what was going on. She had only seen him once before, at lunch, but she remembered him. The patient, her temporary neighbor who rapped on the wall every time she turned the radio up a little, was someone she disliked so strongly that Ruzena perceived everything about the woman with attentive loathing.

The man's face displeased her. It looked ironic to her, and she detested irony. She always thought that irony (all forms of irony) was like an armed guard posted at the entrance to her future, scrutinizing her with an inquisitive eye and rejecting her with a shake of the head. She stuck out her chest, deciding to pass in front of the man with all the provocative arrogance of her breasts, all the pride of her belly.

And the man (she was watching him only out of the corner of her eye) suddenly said in a tender, gentle voice: "Come here, come over here . . ."

At first she didn't understand why he was addressing her. The tenderness in his voice puzzled her, and she didn't know how to respond. But then she turned around and caught sight of a heavy boxer dog with a humanly ugly mug following at her heels.

Jakub's voice attracted the dog. He took him by the collar: "Come with me or you don't stand a chance." The dog lifted his trusting head to the man, his tongue hanging like a cheery little flag.

It was a moment filled with ridiculous, trivial, but obvious humiliation: the man had noticed neither her provocative arrogance nor her pride. She had thought he was talking to her, and he was talking to a dog. She passed in front of him and stopped on the broad front steps of the Richmond.

Two old men armed with poles came rushing across the park toward Jakub. She watched the scene spitefully, unable to keep from taking the old men's side.

Jakub was leading the dog by the collar toward the hotel steps when one of the old men shouted: "Release that dog at once!"

And the other old man: "In the name of the law!"

Jakub pretended not to notice the old men and kept going, but behind him a pole slowly descended alongside his body and the wire loop wavered clumsily over the boxer's head.

Jakub grabbed the end of the pole and brusquely pushed it aside.

A third old man ran up and shouted: "It's an attack on law and order! I'm going to call the police!"

And the high-pitched voice of another old man complained: "He ran on the grass! He ran in the playground, where it's prohibited! He pissed in the kids' sandbox! Do you like dogs more than children?"

Ruzena was watching the scene from the top of the

steps, and the pride that a moment before she had felt only in her belly flowed throughout her body, filling her with defiant strength. Jakub and the dog came up the steps near her, and she said: "It's not allowed to take a dog inside."

Jakub answered her calmly, but she could no longer back down. Her legs apart, she planted herself in front of the Richmond's wide doorway and insisted: "This is a hotel for patients, not a hotel for dogs. Dogs are prohibited here."

"Why don't you get a pole with a loop too, young lady?" said Jakub, trying to go through the doorway with the dog.

Ruzena caught in Jakub's words the irony she so detested and that sent her back where she had come from, back where she did not want to be. Anger blurred her sight. She grabbed hold of the dog by the collar. Now they were both holding him. Jakub was pulling him in and she was pulling him out.

Jakub seized Ruzena's wrist and pried her fingers loose from the collar with such violence that she staggered.

"You'd rather see poodles in cradles than babies!" she shouted after him.

Jakub turned around and their eyes met, joined by sudden, naked hatred.

8

The boxer scampered around the room curiously, unaware that he had just escaped danger. Jakub stretched out on the daybed, wondering what to do with him. He liked the lively, good-natured dog. The insouciance with which, in a few minutes, he had made himself at home in a strange room and struck up a friendship with a strange man was nearly suspicious and seemed to verge on stupidity. After sniffing all corners of the room, he leaped up on the daybed and lay down beside Jakub. Jakub was startled, but he welcomed without reservation this sign of camaraderie. He put his hand on the dog's back and felt with delight the warmth of the animal's body. He had always liked dogs. They were familiar, affectionate, devoted, and at the same time entirely incomprehensible. We will never know what actually goes on in the heads and hearts of these confident, merry emissaries from incomprehensible nature.

He scratched the dog's back and thought about the scene he had just witnessed. The old men armed with long poles merged in his mind with prison guards, examining magistrates, and informers who spied on neighbors to see if they talked politics while shopping. What drove such people to their sinister occupations? Spite? Certainly, but also the desire for order. Because the desire for order tries to transform the human world into an inorganic reign in which everything goes well, everything functions as a subject of an impersonal will. The desire for order is at the same time a desire for death, because life is a perpetual violation of order. Or, inversely, the desire for order is the virtuous pretext by which man's hatred for man justifies its crimes.

Then he thought of the blonde young woman who tried to prevent him from entering the Richmond with the dog, and he felt a painful hatred for her. The old men armed with poles didn't irritate him, he knew them well, he took them into account, he never doubted they existed and had to go on existing and would always be his persecutors. But that young woman, she was his eternal defeat. She was pretty, and she had appeared on the scene not as a persecutor but as a spectator who, fascinated by the spectacle, identified with the persecutors. Jakub was always horror-stricken by the idea that onlookers are ready to restrain the victim during an execution. For, with time, the hangman has become someone near at hand, a familiar figure, while the persecuted one has taken on something of an aristocratic smell. The soul of the crowd, which formerly identified with the miserable persecuted ones, today identifies with the misery of the persecutors. Because to hunt men in our century is to hunt the privileged: those who read books or own a dog.

He felt the animal's warm body under his hand, and he realized that the blonde young woman had come to announce to him, as a secret sign, that he would never be liked in this country and that she, the people's messenger, would always be ready to hold him down so as to offer him up to the men threatening him with poles with wire loops. He hugged the dog and pressed him close. He mused that he could not leave him here at risk, that he must take him along far away from this country as a souvenir of persecution, as one of those who had escaped. Then he realized that he was hiding this merry pooch here as if he were an outlaw fleeing the police, and this notion seemed comic to him.

Someone knocked at the door, and Dr. Skreta entered: "You're finally back, and it's about time. I've been looking for you all afternoon. What have you been up to?"

"I went to see Olga, and then . . ." He started to tell about the dog, but Skreta interrupted him:

"I should have known. Wasting time like that when we've got a lot of things to discuss! I've already told Bertlef you're here, and I've arranged for him to invite both of us."

At that moment the dog jumped off the daybed, went over to the doctor, stood up on his hind legs, and put his front legs on Skreta's chest. He scratched the dog on the nape of the neck. "Yes, yes, Bob, you're a good dog . . ." he said, not surprised to see him there.

"His name is Bob?"

"Yes, it's Bob," said Skreta, and he told him that the dog belonged to the owner of an inn in the forest nearby; everyone knew the dog, because he roamed everywhere.

The dog understood that they were talking about

him, and this pleased him. He wagged his tail and tried to lick Skreta's face.

"You're shrewd psychologically," said the doctor. "You have to study Bertlef in depth for me today. I don't know how to handle him. I've got great plans for him."

"To sell his pious pictures?"

"Pious pictures, that's silly," said Skreta. "This is about something much more important. I want him to adopt me."

"Adopt you?"

"Adopt me as a son. It's vital to me. If I become his adopted son, I'll automatically acquire American citizenship."

"You want to emigrate?"

"No. I'm engaged in long-term experiments here, and I don't want to interrupt them. By the way, I have to talk to you about that too today, because I need you for these experiments. With American citizenship, I'd also get an American passport, and I could travel freely all over the world. You know very well that otherwise it's difficult to leave this country. And I want very much to go to Iceland."

"Why exactly Iceland?"

"Because it has the best salmon fishing," said Skreta. And he went on: "What complicates things a bit is that Bertlef is only fifteen years older than I am. I have to explain to him that adoptive fatherhood is a legal status that has nothing to do with biological fatherhood, and that theoretically he could be my adoptive father even if he were younger than I. Maybe he'll understand this, though he has a very young wife. She's one of my patients. By the way, she'll be arriving here the day after tomorrow. I've sent Suzy to Prague to meet her when she lands."

"Does Suzy know about your plan?"

"Of course. I urged her at all costs to gain her future mother-in-law's friendship."

"And the American? What does he say about it?"

"That's just what's most difficult. The man can't understand it if I don't spell it out for him. That's why I need you, to study him and tell me how to handle him."

Skreta looked at his watch and announced that Bertlef was waiting for them.

"But what are we going to do with Bob?" asked Jakub.

"How come you brought him here?" said Skreta.

Jakub explained to his friend how he had saved the dog's life, but Skreta was immersed in his thoughts and listened to him absentmindedly. After Jakub had finished, he said: "The innkeeper's wife is one of my patients. Two years ago she gave birth to a beautiful baby. They love Bob, you should bring him back to them tomorrow. Meanwhile, let's give him a sleeping tablet so he won't bother us."

He took a tube out of his pocket and shook out a tablet. He called the dog over, opened his jaws, and dropped the tablet down his gullet.

"In a minute, he'll be sleeping sweetly," he said, and he left the room with Jakub.

9

Bertlef welcomed his two visitors, and Jakub ran his eyes over the room. Then he went over to the painting of the bearded saint: "I've heard that you paint," he said to Bertlef.

"Yes," Bertlef replied, "that is Saint Lazarus, my patron saint."

"Why did you paint a blue halo?" asked Jakub, showing his surprise.

"I am glad you asked me that question. As a rule people look at a painting and don't even know what they are seeing. I made the halo blue simply because in reality halos are blue."

Jakub again showed surprise, and Bertlef went on: "People who become attached to God with a particularly powerful love are rewarded by experiencing a sacred joy that flows through their entire being and radiates out from there. The light of this divine joy is soft and peaceful, and its color is the celestial azure."

"Wait a moment," Jakub interrupted. "Are you saying that halos are more than a symbol?"

"Certainly," said Bertlef. "But you should not imagine that they emanate continuously from saints' heads and that saints go around in the world like itinerant lanterns. Of course not. It is only at certain moments of intense inner joy that their brows give off a bluish light. In the first centuries after the death of Jesus, in an era when saints were numerous and there were many people who knew them well, no one had the slightest doubt about the color of halos, and on all the paintings and frescoes of that time you can see that the halos are blue. It was only in the fifth century that painters started little by little to depict them in other colors, such as orange or yellow. Much later, in Gothic painting, there are only golden halos. This was more decorative and better conveyed the terrestrial power and glory of the church. But that halo no more resembled the true halo than the church of the time resembled the early church."

"That's something I was unaware of," said Jakub, and Bertlef went over to the liquor cabinet. He conferred with his two visitors for a few moments about what to drink. When he had poured cognac into the three glasses, he turned to the physician: "Please don't forget about that unhappy expectant father. It is very important to me!"

Skreta assured Bertlef that it would all end well, and Jakub then asked what they were talking about. After they told him (let us appreciate the graceful discretion of the two men, who, even though it was only Jakub with them, mentioned no names), he expressed great pity for the unfortunate begetter: "Which of us hasn't lived through this martyrdom! It's one of life's great trials. Those who give in and become fathers against their will are doomed forever by their defeat. They become spiteful, like all losers, and they wish the same fate on everyone else."

"My friend!" Bertlef exclaimed. "You are speaking

in the company of a happy father! If you stayed here for another day or two, you would see my son, a beautiful child, and you would take back what you have just said!"

"I wouldn't take anything back," said Jakub, "because you didn't become a father against your will!"

"Certainly not. I became a father by my own free will and by the good will of Doctor Skreta."

The doctor nodded with an air of satisfaction and declared that he too had a notion of fatherhood different from Jakub's, as shown, by the way, by the blessed state of his dear Suzy. "The only thing," he added, "that puzzles me a bit about procreation is how senselessly parents choose each other. It's incredible what hideous-looking individuals decide to procreate. They probably imagine that the burden of ugliness will be lighter if they share it with their descendants."

Bertlef called Dr. Skreta's viewpoint aesthetic racism: "Don't forget that not only was Socrates ugly but also that many famous women lovers did not distinguish themselves at all by their physical perfection. Aesthetic racism is almost always a sign of inexperience. Those who have not made their way far enough into the world of amorous delights judge women only by what can be seen. But those who really know women understand that the eye reveals only a minute fraction of what a woman can offer us. When God bade mankind be fruitful and multiply, Doctor, He was thinking of the ugly as well as of the beautiful. I am convinced, I might add, that the aesthetic criterion does not come from God but from the devil. In paradise no distinction was made between ugliness and beauty."

Jakub reentered the conversation, asserting that aesthetic considerations played no part in the loathing he felt for procreation. "But I can cite ten other reasons for not being a father."

"What are they? I am curious."

"First of all, I don't like motherhood," said Jakub, and he broke off pensively. "Our century has already unmasked all myths. Childhood has long ceased to be an age of innocence. Freud discovered infant sexuality and told us all about Oedipus. Only Jocasta remains untouchable; no one dares tear off her veil. Motherhood is the last and greatest taboo, the one that harbors the most grievous curse. There is no stronger bond than the one that shackles mother to child. This bond cripples the child's soul forever and prepares for the mother, when her son has grown up, the most cruel of all the griefs of love. I say that motherhood is a curse, and I refuse to contribute to it."

"Next!" said Bertlef.

"Another reason I don't want to add to the number of mothers," said Jakub with some embarrassment, "is that I love the female body, and I am disgusted by the thought of my beloved's breast becoming a milk-bag."

"Next!" said Bertlef.

"The doctor here will certainly confirm that physicians and nurses treat women hospitalized after an aborted pregnancy more harshly than those who have given birth, and show some contempt toward them even though they themselves will, at least once in their lives, need a similar operation. But for them it's a reflex stronger than any kind of thought, because the cult of procreation is an imperative of nature. That's why it's useless to look for the slightest rational argument in natalist propaganda. Do you perhaps think it's the voice of Jesus you're hearing in the natalist morality of the church? Do you think it's the voice of Marx you're hearing in the natalist propaganda of the Communist state? Impelled merely by the desire to perpetuate the species, mankind will end up smothering itself on its small planet. But the natalist propaganda mill grinds on, and the public is moved to tears by pictures of nursing mothers and infants making faces. It disgusts me. It chills me to think that, along with millions of other enthusiasts, I could be bending over a cradle with a silly smile."

"Next!" said Bertlef.

"And of course I also have to ask myself what sort of world I'd be sending my child into. School soon takes him away to stuff his head with the falsehoods I've fought in vain against all my life. Should I see my son become a conformist fool? Or should I instill my own ideas into him and see him suffer because he'll be dragged into the same conflicts I was?"

"Next!" said Bertlef.

"And of course I also have to think of myself. In this country children pay for their parents' disobedience, and parents for their children's disobedience. How many young people have been denied education because their parents fell into disgrace? And how many parents have chosen permanent cowardice for the sole purpose of preventing harm to their children? Anyone who wants to preserve at least some freedom here shouldn't have children," Jakub said, and fell into silence.

"You still need five more reasons to complete your decalogue," said Bertlef.

"The last reason carries so much weight that it counts for five," said Jakub. "Having a child is to show an absolute accord with mankind. If I have a child, it's as though I'm saying: I was born and have tasted life and declare it so good that it merits being duplicated."

"And you have not found life to be good?" asked Bertlef.

Jakub tried to be precise, and said cautiously: "All I know is that I could never say with complete conviction: Man is a wonderful being and I want to reproduce him."

"That's because you've only known life in its worst aspect," said Dr. Skreta. "You've never known how to live. You've always thought that it was your duty to be, as they say, in the thick of things. In the core of reality. But what was that reality for you? Politics. And politics is what is least essential and least precious in life. Politics is the dirty foam on the surface of the river, while the life of the river is lived much deeper. The study of female fertility has been going on for thousands of years. It's had a solid, steady history. And it's quite indifferent to which government it is that happens to be in power. When I put on a rubber glove and examine a female organ, I'm much nearer the core of life than you, who nearly lost your life because you were concerned about the good of humanity."

Instead of protesting Jakub agreed with his friend's reproaches, and Dr. Skreta, feeling encouraged, went on: "Archimedes with his circles, Michelangelo with his block of stone, Pasteur with his test tubes—they and they alone have transformed human life and made real history, while the politicians . . ." Skreta paused and waved his hand scornfully.

"While the politicians?" asked Jakub, and went on: "I'll tell you. If science and art are in fact the proper, real arenas of history, politics on the contrary is the closed scientific laboratory where unprecedented experiments are conducted on mankind. There human guinea pigs are hurled through trap doors and then brought back onto the stage, tempted by applause and terrified by the gallows, denounced and forced to denounce. I worked in that lab as an assistant, but I also served there several times as a victim of vivisection. I know that I created nothing of value there (no more than those who worked with me did), but I probably came to understand better than others what man is."

"I understand you," said Bertlef, "and I too know that laboratory, even though I never worked as an assistant but always as a guinea pig. I was in Germany when the war broke out. The woman I was in love with at the time denounced me to the Gestapo. They had come to her and shown her a photo of me in bed with another woman. She was hurt by it, and, as you know, love often takes on the features of hate. I went to prison with the strange sensation of having been led there by love. Is it not wonderful to find oneself in the hands of the Gestapo and to realize that this, in fact, is the privilege of a man who is loved too much?"

Jakub replied: "Something that always utterly disgusts me about mankind is seeing how its cruelty, its baseness, and its stupidity manage to wear the lyrical mask. She sends you to your death, and she experiences it as a romantic feat of wounded love. And you mount the scaffold because of an ordinary narrow-minded woman, feeling that you are playing a role in a tragedy Shakespeare wrote for you."

"After the war she came to me in tears," Bertlef went on, as though he had not heard Jakub's objection. "I told her: 'Don't worry, Bertlef is never vindictive.'"

"You know," said Jakub, "I often think about King Herod. You know the story. It's said that when he learned about the birth of the future king of the Jews, he was afraid he'd lose his throne, and he had all the newborns murdered. Personally I have a different view of Herod, even though I know it's only an imaginary game. To my mind Herod was an educated, wise, and very generous king, who had worked for a long time in the laboratory of politics and had learned much about life and mankind. He came to think that perhaps man should not have been created. His doubt, I might add, was not so uncalled-for and reprehensible. If I'm not mistaken, even the Lord had doubts about mankind and thought of destroying this part of His work."

"Yes," Bertlef agreed, "it is in the sixth chapter of Genesis: 'I will destroy man whom I have created . . . for it repenteth me that I have made him.'"

"And perhaps it was only a moment of weakness on the Lord's part finally to have permitted Noah to take refuge in his ark in order to start afresh the history of man. Can we be sure that God never regretted this weakness? But whether He regretted it or not, there was nothing more to do. God can't make Himself ridiculous by constantly changing His decisions. But what if it was He who put the idea into Herod's head? Can that be ruled out?"

Bertlef shrugged his shoulders and said nothing.

"Herod was a king. He was not just responsible for himself alone. He couldn't tell himself, as I do: Let others do what they want, I refuse to procreate. Herod was a king and knew that he had to decide not only for himself but also for others, and he decided on behalf of all mankind that man would no longer reproduce. This is how the massacre of the newborns came about. His motives were not as vile as the ones tradition attributes to him. Herod was driven by a most generous wish finally to free the world from mankind's clutches."

"Your interpretation of Herod pleases me greatly," said Bertlef. "It pleases me so much that from now on I shall see the Massacre of the Innocents as you do. But don't forget that at the very moment Herod decided that mankind would cease to exist, there was born in

Bethlehem a little boy who was to elude the king's knife. And this child grew up and told people that only one thing was needed to make life worth living: to love one another. Herod was probably better educated and more experienced. Jesus was certainly wet behind the ears and did not know much about life. All his teachings might be explained by his youth and inexperience. By his naïveté, if you wish. And yet he possessed the truth."

"The truth? Who has proved this truth?" Jakub asked sharply.

"No one," said Bertlef. "No one has proved it, and no one ever will prove it. Jesus loved his Father so much that he could not admit his Father's work was bad. He was not led to this conclusion by reason but by love. This is why only our hearts can bring the quarrel between Jesus and Herod to a close. Is it worth being a man, yes or no? I have no proof of it, but, along with Jesus, I believe the answer is yes." That said, he turned with a smile to Dr. Skreta: "That is why I sent my wife here to take the cure under the direction of Doctor Skreta, who to my mind is one of the holy disciples of Jesus, for he knows how to perform miracles and bring back to life women's dormant wombs. I drink to his health!"

10

Jakub had always treated Olga with paternal responsibility and playfully liked to call himself her "old gentleman." She knew, however, that he had many women with whom things were entirely different, and she envied them. But today, for the first time, she thought there was really something old about Jakub. In the way he behaved with her, she sensed the mustiness that for the young emanates from the generation of their elders.

Old men are recognizable by their habit of bragging about past sufferings and making a museum of them (ah, these sad museums have so few visitors!). Olga realized that she was the most important living object in Jakub's museum and that Jakub's generously altruistic attitude toward her was meant to move visitors to tears.

Today too the most precious nonliving object in the museum had been revealed to her: the pale-blue tablet. Not long before, when he had unfolded in her presence the piece of paper the tablet was wrapped in, she had been surprised by not feeling the slightest emotion. Though she understood Jakub's contemplation of suicide in a bad time, she found the solemnity with which he let her know about it ridiculous. She found it ridiculous that he had unfolded the tissue paper so cautiously, as if the tablet were a precious diamond. And she didn't see why he wanted to give the poison back to

Dr. Skreta on the day of his departure, since he had maintained that every adult should under all circumstances be in control of his own death. If, once he was abroad, he were stricken by cancer, would he not need the poison? No, for Jakub the tablet was not simply poison, it was a symbolic prop he now wanted to return to the high priest in a religious service. It was enough to make you laugh.

She left the baths and headed toward the Richmond. Despite all her disillusioned reflections, she looked forward to seeing Jakub. She had a great desire to desecrate his museum, to function in it no longer as an object but as a woman. She was thus a bit disappointed to find a note on his door asking her to join him in the room next door, where he was waiting for her with Bertlef and Dr. Skreta. The thought of being in the company of others made her lose heart, all the more so since she didn't know Bertlef, and Dr. Skreta usually treated her with friendly but obvious indifference.

Bertlef quickly made her forget her shyness. He introduced himself with a deep bow and chided Dr. Skreta for not having acquainted him sooner with such an interesting woman.

Skreta responded that Jakub had asked him to look after the young woman, and he had deliberately refrained from introducing her to Bertlef because he knew that no woman could resist him.

Bertlef greeted this excuse with a satisfied smile. Then he picked up the telephone receiver to order dinner.

"It's incredible," said Dr. Skreta, "how our friend

manages to live affluently in this hole where there's not a single restaurant that serves a decent meal."

Bertlef dug his hand into an open cigar box, beside the telephone, which was filled with half-dollar pieces: "Avarice is a sin," he said, and smiled.

Jakub remarked that he had never before met anyone who believed so fervently in God while knowing so well how to enjoy life.

"That is probably because you have never before met a true Christian. The word of the Gospel, as you know, is a message of joy. The enjoyment of life is the most important teaching of Jesus."

Olga considered this an opportunity to enter the conversation: "Insofar as I can trust what my teachers said, Christians saw earthly life as a vale of tears and rejoiced in the idea that true life would begin for them after death."

"My dear young lady," Bertlef said, "never believe teachers."

"And what the saints all did," Olga went on, "was to renounce life. Instead of making love they flagellated themselves; instead of discussing things as you and I are doing they retreated to hermitages; and instead of ordering dinner by telephone they chewed roots."

"You don't understand anything about saints, my dear. These people were immensely attached to the pleasures of life. But they attained them by other means. In your opinion, what is man's supreme pleasure? You could try to guess, but you would be deceiving yourself, because you are not sincere enough. This is not a reproach, for sincerity requires self-knowledge and self-knowledge is the fruit of age. How could a young woman like you, who radiates youthfulness, be sincere? She cannot be sincere because she does not even know what there is within her. But if she did know, she would have to admit along with me that the greatest pleasure is to be admired. Do you agree?"

Olga replied that she knew of greater pleasures.

"No," said Bertlef. "Take for instance your famous runner, the one every child here knows about because he won three Olympic events. Do you think he renounced life? And yet instead of chatting, making love, and eating well, he surely had to spend his time constantly running round and round a stadium. His training very much resembled what our most celebrated saints did. Saint Makarios of Alexandria, when he was in the desert, regularly refilled a basket with sand, put it on his back, and traveled endless distances in this way day after day until he dropped from total exhaustion. But both for your runner and for Saint Makarios, there was surely a great reward that amply repaid them for all their efforts. Do you know what it is to hear the applause in an immense Olympic stadium? There is no greater joy! Saint Makarios of Alexandria knew why he carried a basket of sand on his back. The glory of his desert marathons soon spread throughout Christendom. And Saint Makarios was like your runner. Your runner, too, first won the five-thousand-meter race, then the ten-thousand-meter, and finally nothing sufficed for him but to win the marathon as well. The desire for admiration is insatiable. Saint Makarios went to a monastery in Thebes without making himself known and asked to be accepted as a member. Then, when the Lenten fast began, came his hour of glory. All the monks fasted sitting down, but he remained standing for the entire forty-day fast! You have no idea what a triumph that was! Or remember Saint Simeon Stylites! In the desert he built a pillar with a narrow platform on top. There was no room to sit on it, he had to stand. And he remained standing there for the rest of his life, and all Christendom enthusiastically admired this man's incredible record, which seemed to exceed human limits. Saint Simeon Stylites was the Gagarin of the fifth century. Can you imagine the happiness of Saint Geneviève of Paris the day she learned from a Welsh trading mission that Saint Simeon Stylites had heard of her and blessed her from atop his pillar? And why do you think he wanted to set a record? Because he didn't care about life and mankind? Don't be naïve! The church fathers knew very well that Saint Simeon Stylites was vain, and they put him to the test. In the name of their spiritual authority they ordered him to descend from his pillar and retire from competition. It was a harsh blow to Saint Simeon Stylites! But he was either wise or cunning enough to obey them. The church fathers were not hostile to his record-setting, but they wanted to be certain that Saint Simeon's vanity did not prevail over his sense of discipline. As soon as they saw him sadly descending from his perch, they ordered him to climb back up, ensuring that Saint Simeon could die on his pillar surrounded by the love and admiration of the world."

Olga listened attentively, and upon hearing Bertlef's last words she began to laugh.

"That tremendous desire for admiration has nothing laughable about it, I find it rather moving," said Bertlef. "Someone who desires admiration is attached to his fellow men, he cares about them, he cannot live without them. Saint Simeon Stylites is alone in the desert on a square meter of pillar. And yet he is with all mankind! He imagines millions of eyes raised toward him. He is present in millions of thoughts, and this delights him. It is a great example of love for mankind and love for life. You would not suspect, dear young lady, to what extent Simeon Stylites continues to live in every one of us. And to this day he is the better of the polarities of our being."

Someone knocked at the door, and in came a waiter pushing a cart loaded with food. He spread a tablecloth and set the table. Bertlef dug into the cigar box and stuffed a fistful of coins into the waiter's pocket. Then they all began to eat, with the waiter behind them pouring wine and serving the various dishes.

Bertlef commented greedily on the tastiness of each dish, and Skreta remarked that he didn't know how long it had been since he had had such a good meal. "Maybe the last time was when my mother was still cooking for me, but I was still little then. I've been an orphan since the age of five. After that, the world around me was a strange world, and the cooking also seemed strange to me. The love of food arises from the love of the nearest and dearest."

"Quite right," said Bertlef, lifting a mouthful of beef to his lips.

"A forsaken child loses its appetite," Skreta went on. "Believe me, to this day I feel bad about having no father or mother. Believe me, to this day, and as old as I am, I'd give anything to have a papa."

"You overestimate family affinities," said Bertlef. "Everyone is your nearest and dearest. Don't forget what Jesus said when they tried to call him back to his mother and brothers. He pointed to his disciples and said: 'Here are my mother and my brothers.'"

"And yet the Holy Church," Dr. Skreta ventured to reply, "didn't have the slightest desire to abolish the family or to replace it with a community open to everyone."

"There is a difference between the Holy Church and Jesus. And to my mind Saint Paul, if you will allow me to say so, is not only the successor but also the falsifier of Jesus. First there is the sudden change from Saul to Paul! As if we have not known enough of those passionate fanatics who trade one faith for another in the course of a night! And let no one tell me that the fanatics are guided by love! They are moralists muttering their ten commandments. But Jesus was not a moralist. Remember what he said when they reproached him for not celebrating the Sabbath: 'The Sabbath was made for man, and not man for the Sabbath.' Jesus loved women! And can you picture Saint Paul with the features of a lover? Saint Paul would condemn me because I love women. But Jesus would not. I don't see anything bad about loving women, many women, and about being loved by women, many women." Bertlef smiled, and his smile expressed great self-satisfaction: "My friends, I have not had an easy life, and more than once I have looked death in the eye. But in one thing God has shown himself to be generous to me. I have had a multitude of women, and they have loved me."

The guests finished their meal, and the waiter was beginning to clear the table when there was another knock at the door. It was weak, shy knocking, as if begging for encouragement. "Come in!" said Bertlef.

The door opened, and a child came in. It was a little girl about five years old; she was wearing a ruffled white dress belted with a broad white ribbon tied in back with a huge bow looking like a pair of wings. She was holding a flower by the stem: a large dahlia. Seeing in the room so many people who all seemed to be staring dumbfounded at her, she stopped, not daring to go farther.

Then Bertlef, beaming, stood up and said: "Don't be afraid, little angel, come on in."

And the child, as though she were seeing support in Bertlef's smile, burst out laughing and ran over to Bertlef, who accepted the flower and kissed her on the forehead.

The guests and the waiter watched this scene with surprise. With the huge white bow on her back, the child really did look like a little angel. And Bertlef, bending over her with the dahlia in his hand, made one think of the Baroque statues of saints to be seen in the country's small towns.

"Dear friends," he said, turning to his guests, "I have had a very pleasant time with you, and I hope that you too have enjoyed yourselves. I would gladly stay with you late into the night, but as you can see, I am unable to. This beautiful angel has come to summon me to a person who is waiting for me. I told you that life has struck me with all kinds of blows, but women have loved me."

Bertlef held the dahlia against his chest with one hand and with the other touched the little girl's shoulder. He bowed to his small group of guests. Olga thought him ridiculously theatrical, and she was delighted to see him go and that, finally, she would soon be alone with Jakub.

Bertlef turned around and, taking the little girl's hand, headed toward the door. But before leaving the room he bent over the cigar box to fill his pocket with an ample fistful of coins.

11

The waiter stacked the dirty dishes and empty bottles on the cart, and when he had left the room, Olga asked: "Who is that little girl?"

"I've never seen her before," said Skreta.

"She really did have the look of a little angel," said Jakub.

"An angel who procures mistresses for him?" said Olga.

"Yes," said Jakub. "A procurer and go-between angel. It's exactly how I picture his guardian angel."

"I don't know if she's an angel," said Skreta, "but what's curious is that I've never seen this little girl before, although I know nearly everybody around here."

"In that case there's only one explanation," said Jakub. "She's not of this world."

"Whether she's an angel or the chambermaid's daughter, I can guarantee you," said Olga, "that he hasn't gone to meet a woman! He's a terribly vain character, and all he does is brag."

"I find him likable," said Jakub.

"He might well be," said Olga, "but I still insist he's the vainest kind of character. I'm willing to bet that an hour before we arrived he gave some of those fifty-cent coins to that little girl and asked her to come here at a certain time holding a flower. Believers have a great talent for staging miracles."

"I very much hope you're right," said Dr. Skreta. "Because Mister Bertlef is actually a very sick man, and a night of love would expose him to great danger."

"You see, I was right. All his hints about women are just bluster."

"My dear young woman," said Dr. Skreta, "I'm his

physician and his friend, and yet I'm not so sure. I don't know."

"Is he really so ill?" asked Jakub.

"Why do you think he's been staying here for nearly a year now, and his young wife, to whom he's very attached, comes to see him only now and again?"

"And all of a sudden it's a bit dreary here without him," said Jakub.

True, all three suddenly felt orphaned and not at home in the room, and they had no wish to stay any longer.

Skreta got up from his chair: "You and I are going to take Miss Olga home, and then we'll go for a walk. We've got a lot of things to discuss."

Olga protested: "I don't want to go to sleep yet!"

"On the contrary, it's high time. I'm ordering you to as your physician," Skreta said sternly.

They left the Richmond and headed across the park. On the way Olga found an opportunity to say softly to Jakub: "I wanted to spend the evening with you . . ."

But Jakub merely shrugged his shoulders, for Skreta was imperiously imposing his will. They escorted the young woman to Karl Marx House, and in his friend's presence Jakub did not even pat her on the head, as he usually did. The doctor's antipathy toward her plumlike breasts had deterred him. He saw the disappointment in Olga's face and was annoyed with himself for distressing her.

"So what do you think?" asked Skreta when he found himself alone with his friend on the path. "You heard me say I need a father. It would have wrung tears from a stone. But he started talking about Saint Paul! Is it really so hard for him to understand? For two years now I've been telling him I'm an orphan, two years praising the advantages of an American passport. I've alluded a thousand times in passing to various adoption cases. I figured all these allusions would have given him the idea of adopting me long ago."

"He's too absorbed in himself," said Jakub.

"That's so," Skreta agreed.

"If he's seriously ill, that's not surprising," said Jakub. "Is he really as sick as you said he is?"

"It's really worse," said Skreta. "Six months ago he had his second and very serious heart attack, and since then he hasn't been allowed to travel far, and he lives here like a prisoner. His life hangs by a thread. And he knows it."

"You see," said Jakub, "in that case you should have realized a long time ago that the allusions method is no good, because any allusion only causes him to think about himself. You should make your request directly. He certainly will agree, because he likes to please people. It fits with his idea of himself. He wants to give people pleasure."

"You're a genius!" Skreta exclaimed, coming to a stop. "It's simple once you think of it, and exactly right! Like an idiot I've wasted two years of my life because I didn't know how to figure him out! I've spent two years of my life going about it in roundabout ways!

And it's your fault, because you should have advised me long ago."

"You should have asked me long ago!"

"You haven't come to see me for two years!"

The two friends strolled on in the dark park, breathing in the crisp early autumn air.

"I made him a father," said Skreta, "so maybe I deserve his making me his son!"

Jakub agreed.

"What's unfortunate," Skreta went on after a long silence, "is that one is surrounded by idiots. Is there anyone in this town I can ask for advice? Merely by being born intelligent, you right away find yourself in absolute exile. I don't think about anything else, because it's my specialty: mankind produces an incredible quantity of idiots. The more stupid the individual, the more he wants to procreate. The perfect creatures at most engender a single child, and the best of them, like you, decide not to procreate at all. That's a disaster. And I spend my time dreaming of a world a man would come into not among strangers but among brothers."

Jakub listened to Skreta's speech without finding much of interest in it.

Skreta went on: "Don't think those are just words! I'm not a politician but a physician, and the word 'brother' has an exact meaning for me. Brothers are those who have at least a mother or a father in common. All of Solomon's sons, even though they had a hundred different mothers, were brothers. That must have been marvelous! What do you think?"

Jakub breathed the crisp air and could not think of anything to say.

"Of course," Skreta went on, "it's very hard to force people while they're having sex to take an interest in future generations. But that's not what it's about. In our century there should really be other ways of solving the problem of rational procreation of children. We can't go on forever mixing up love and procreation."

Jakub approved of that idea.

"But you're only interested in detaching love from procreation," said Skreta. "For me, instead, it's a matter of detaching procreation from love. I want to initiate you into my project. It was my semen in that test tube."

This time he got Jakub's attention.

"What do you say to that?"

"It's a marvelous idea," said Jakub.

"It's extraordinary!" said Skreta. "By this procedure I've already cured quite a few women. Don't forget that many women can't have children only because it's the husbands who are sterile. I have a large clientele from all over the country, and for the last four years I've been in charge of gynecological examinations at the town clinic. It's no big deal to fill a syringe from a test tube and then deposit the seminal fluid into a woman being examined."

"So how many children do you have?"

"I've been doing this for several years, but I can only make a very approximate tally. I can't always be certain I'm the father because my patients are, so to speak, unfaithful to me with their husbands. And besides, they go back home, and it happens that I don't find out if the treatment succeeded. Things are clearer with the local patients."

Skreta fell silent, and Jakub gave himself up to tender reverie. Skreta's project delighted and moved him, for in it he recognized his old friend the incorrigible dreamer: "It must be terrific to have children with so many women," he said.

"And they're all brothers," Skreta added.

They strolled on, breathing the fragrant air in silence. Then Skreta resumed talking: "You know, I often tell myself that even though there are a lot of things here we don't like, we're responsible for this country. It infuriates me that I can't travel abroad freely, but I could never defame my country. I'd have to defame myself first. And which one of us has ever done anything to make this country better? Which one of us has ever done anything to make it possible to live here? To make it be a country where you could feel at home? Simply to feel at home . . ." Skreta now spoke more softly, tenderly: "Feeling at home is being among one's own. And because you said you're leaving, I've thought that I have to persuade you to take part in my project. I've got a test tube for you. You'll be abroad, and your children will be brought into the world here. And in ten or twenty years you'll see what a splendid country this will be!"

There was a round moon in the sky (it will stay there until the last night of our story, which we could therefore call a *lunar story*), and Dr. Skreta accompanied Jakub back to the Richmond. "You don't have to leave tomorrow," he said.

"I have to. They're waiting for me," said Jakub, but he knew that he would let himself be persuaded.

"Nonsense," said Skreta. "I'm glad you like my project. Tomorrow we're going to discuss it in detail."

Fourth Day

1

Mrs. Klima was getting ready to leave, but her husband was still in bed.

"Don't you also have to leave this morning?" she asked him.

"Why hurry? I've got plenty of time to get to those morons," Klima replied. He yawned and turned over.

He had announced to her two days before, in the middle of Tuesday night, that at the exhausting conference he had just come back from he had been pressured to help amateur bands and thus forced into giving a concert in a small spa town on Thursday evening with a jazz-playing pharmacist and physician. He had shouted all this angrily, but Mrs. Klima looked him in the face and clearly saw that his indignant curses were insincere, that there was no concert and Klima had invented it only to provide himself some time for one of his love intrigues. She could read everything on his face; he could never hide anything from her. Now, as he swore, yawned, and turned over, she realized instantly that he was doing so not out of sleepiness but to hide his face and prevent her from scrutinizing it.

Then she left for work. When, some years earlier, her illness had deprived her of her place in front of the footlights, Klima found her a job at the theater as a secretary. It was not unpleasant, she met interesting people every day, and she was fairly free to arrange her own work schedule. Now she sat down in her office to write several official letters, but she could not manage to concentrate.

Nothing absorbs a human being more completely than jealousy. When Kamila lost her mother a year earlier, it was certainly an event more tragic than one of the trumpeter's escapades. And yet the death of her mother, whom she loved immensely, caused her less pain. The pain of her grief was benignly multicolored: there was sadness in it, and longing, emotion, regret (had Kamila taken sufficient care of her mother? had she neglected her?), even a serene smile. That pain was benignly dispersed in all directions: Kamila's thoughts rebounded from her mother's coffin and flew off toward memories, toward her own childhood and, still further, toward her mother's childhood, they flew off toward dozens of practical concerns, they flew off toward the future, which was wide open and where, as consolation (yes, in those exceptional days her husband was her consolation), Klima's figure stood outlined.

The pain of jealousy, on the contrary, did not move about in space, it turned like a drill on a single point. There was no dispersal. If her mother's death had opened the door to a future (different, more lonely, and also more adult), the suffering caused by her husband's infidelity opened no future at all. Everything was concentrated on a single (and perpetually present) image of an unfaithful body, on a single (and perpetually present) reproach. When she lost her mother, Kamila could listen to music, she could even read; when she was jealous she could do nothing at all.

The day before, she had already gotten the idea of going to the spa town so as to check on the existence of the suspect concert, but she immediately gave it up because she knew that her jealousy would horrify Klima and that she must not overtly reveal it to him. But jealousy ran inside her like a racing engine, and she was unable to resist picking up the telephone and dialing the railroad station. In self-justification she told herself that she was phoning absentmindedly, with no particular intent, because she was unable to concentrate on administrative correspondence.

When she learned that the train departed at eleven, she imagined herself going up and down unfamiliar streets in search of a poster with Klima's name on it, asking at the tourist bureau if they knew about a concert to be given by her husband, being told there is no such concert, and then wandering, wretched and betrayed, through a strange and deserted town. And then she imagined Klima talking about the concert the next day and questioning him about the details. She would look him in the face, listen to his inventions, and drink the poisonous brew of his lies with bitter pleasure.

But she immediately told herself that she should not behave this way. No, she could not spend whole days and weeks spying and nurturing the images of her jealousy. She dreaded losing him, and because of this fear she would end up losing him!

But another voice immediately replied with cunning naïveté: No, she was not going to spy on him! Klima had asserted that he was going to give a concert, and she believed him! It was just because she did not wish to be jealous that she took him seriously, that she accepted his assertions without suspicion! He had said that he was going unhappily, that he was afraid he would be spending a dreary day and evening there! It was thus only to prepare a pleasant surprise for him that she decided to go and join him! When Klima, at the end of the concert, was disgustedly taking his bows and thinking of the exhausting trip home, she would slip onto the foot of the stage, he would see her, and they would both laugh!

She handed the manager the letters she had written with difficulty. They thought well of her at the theater. They appreciated the modesty and friendliness of a famous musician's wife. The sadness that sometimes emanated from her had something disarming about it. The manager could not refuse her anything. She promised to return Friday afternoon and stay late at the theater that day to make up the lost time.

2

It was ten o'clock, and, as she did each day, Olga had just received a large white sheet and a key from Ruzena. She went into a cubicle, took off her clothes, hung them on a hanger, slung the sheet around her like a toga, locked the cubicle, returned the key to Ruzena, and headed for the adjoining room with the pool. She threw the sheet onto the railing and went down the steps into the water, where there were already many women bathing. The pool was not big, but Olga was convinced that swimming was necessary for her health, and so she tried a few strokes. That splashed water into the talkative mouth of one of the ladies. "Are you crazy?" she cried out at Olga testily. "This pool isn't for swimming!"

Women were squatting in the shallow water, huddled up along the wall of the pool like big frogs. Olga was afraid of them. They were all older than she, they were more robust, they had more fat and skin. She thus sat down among them humbled, and stayed motionless and frowning.

Then she suddenly caught sight of a young man at the door; he was short and wore blue jeans and a torn sweater.

"What's that fellow doing here?" she exclaimed.

All the women turned in the direction Olga was looking and started to snicker and squeal.

Just then Ruzena came into the room and shouted:

"We've got visitors. They're going to film you for the news."

The women greeted this with great laughter.

Olga protested: "What is all this?"

"The management gave them permission," said Ruzena.

"I don't care about the management, nobody consulted me!" Olga exclaimed.

The young man in the torn sweater (he had a light meter dangling from his neck) approached the pool and looked at Olga with a grin she found obscene: "Miss, thousands of viewers will go mad for you when they see you on the screen!"

The women responded with a new burst of laughter, and Olga hid her chest with her hands (it was not difficult, for, as we know, her breasts looked like two plums) and huddled behind the others.

Two more fellows in blue jeans moved toward the pool, and the taller one declared: "Please behave just as naturally as you would if we weren't here."

Olga reached out to the railing where her sheet was hanging. Still in the water, she wrapped the sheet around her and then climbed the steps and stood on the tiled floor; the sheet was dripping wet.

"Oh, shit! Don't go yet!" shouted the young man in the torn sweater.

"You have to stay in the pool fifteen minutes more!" Ruzena then shouted.

"She's shy!" came with guffaws from the pool behind Olga's back.

Petr Vácha, DIČ:CZ6307141643
Provozovna-Knihkupectví Na Můstku
Na Příkopě 3
Praha 1 110 00

Účtenka č:2434121/2   16:56

Zboží   Množ. DPH   Celkem

Farewell Waltz /K   1.000   5%   347.00

Celkem Kč s DPH :   347.00

Datum vystavení: 13/09/2004
Datum uskut.zdanit.plnění: 13/09/2004

DPH 5% :   16.52   základ: 330.48

Placeno hotově

Přijato   :   400.00
Vráceno   :   53.00

Vystavil : JAN
Děkujeme za návštěvu.
Tel. 224238292, 2242163?

"She's afraid somebody'll steal her beauty!" said Ruzena.

"Look at her, the princess!" said a voice from the pool.

"Those who don't wish to be filmed of course may go," the tall fellow calmly said.

"The rest of us aren't ashamed! We're beautiful women!" a fat woman said stridently, and the laughter rippled the surface of the water.

"But that young lady can't go! She has to stay in the pool fifteen minutes more!" protested Ruzena as her eyes followed Olga stubbornly heading toward the changing room.

3

No one could blame Ruzena for being in a bad mood. But why was she so irritated by Olga's refusal to let herself be filmed? Why did she identify herself so totally with the mob of fat women who had welcomed the men's arrival with joyful squeals?

And, by the way, why were these fat women squealing so joyfully? Was it because they wanted to display their beauty to the young men and to seduce them?

Surely not. Their conspicuous shamelessness arose precisely from the certainty that they had no seductive beauty at their disposal. They were filled with rancor against youthful women, and hoped by exhibiting their sexually useless bodies to malign and mock female nakedness. They wished to take revenge on and torpedo with the repulsiveness of their bodies the glory of female beauty, for they knew that bodies, whether beautiful or ugly, are ultimately all the same and that the ugly overshadow the beautiful as they whisper in men's ears: Look, this is the truth of the body that bewitches you! Look, this big flabby tit is the same thing as that breast you so madly adore.

The joyful shamelessness of the fat women in the pool was a necrophiliac ring dance around the transience of youth, a ring dance made all the more joyful by the presence in the pool of a young woman to serve as sacrificial victim. When Olga wrapped herself in the sheet they interpreted the gesture as sabotage of their cruel rite, and thus they were furious.

But Ruzena was neither fat nor old, she was actually prettier than Olga! Why then did she show no solidarity with her?

Had she decided to have an abortion and been convinced that happiness with Klima was awaiting her, she would have reacted quite differently. Consciousness of being loved separates a woman from the herd, and Ruzena would have been enraptured by the experience of her inimitable singularity. She would have seen the fat women as enemies and Olga as a sister. She would have come to her aid, as beauty comes to the aid of beauty, happiness to happiness, love to love.

But the night before, Ruzena had slept very poorly and had decided that she could not count on Klima's love, so that everything separating her from the herd seemed to her an illusion. All she had was the burgeoning embryo in her belly, protected by society and tradition. All she had was the glorious universality of female destiny, which promised to fight for her.

And these women in the pool exactly represented femaleness in its universality: the femaleness of eternal childbirth, nursing and withering, the femaleness that snickers at the thought of that fleeting second when a woman believes she is loved and feels she is an inimitable individual.

There is no reconciliation possible between a woman who is convinced she is unique and women who have shrouded themselves in universal female destiny. After a sleepless night heavy with thought, Ruzena took (poor trumpeter!) the side of those women.

4

Jakub was at the wheel, and Bob, sitting beside him on the front seat, kept turning his head to lick his face. Beyond the last houses of the town stood high-rise apartment buildings. They had not been there the year before, and Jakub found them hideous. In the midst of a green landscape they were like brooms in a plant pot. Jakub was stroking Bob, who was looking at the buildings with satisfaction, and he reflected that God had been kind to dogs in not putting a sense of beauty into their heads.

The dog again licked his face (perhaps he felt that Jakub was always thinking about him), and Jakub thought that in his country things were getting neither better nor worse but only more and more ridiculous: he had once been victim of a hunt for humans, and yesterday he witnessed a hunt for dogs that was like the same old play with a new cast. Pensioners took the roles of examining magistrates and prison guards, and the parts of the imprisoned political figures were played by a boxer dog, a mutt, and a dachshund.

He remembered that several years earlier his neighbors had found their cat in front of their door with its legs bound, nails pushed into its eyes, its tongue cut out. Neighborhood kids had been playing adults. Jakub stroked Bob's head and parked the car in front of the inn.

When he stepped out he thought the dog would rush joyfully toward the door of his home. But instead of starting to run, Bob jumped around Jakub, wanting to play. And yet when a voice shouted "Bob!" the dog was off like a shot toward a woman standing in the doorway.

"You're a hopeless vagabond," she said, and she asked Jakub apologetically how long the dog had been bothering him.

When Jakob replied that the dog had spent the night with him and that he had just driven him back home, the woman profusely and noisily thanked him and urged him to come in. She seated him in a special room apparently used for club banquets and rushed off in search of her husband.

She soon came back with a young man who sat down beside Jakub and shook his hand: "You must be a very nice man to drive all the way here just to bring Bob back. He's stupid, and all he does is run around. But we really love him. Would you like something to eat?"

"Yes, thanks," said Jakub, and the woman rushed off to the kitchen. Then Jakub recounted how he had saved Bob from a bunch of pensioners.

"The bastards!" exclaimed the young man, and then, turning toward the kitchen, called out to his wife: "Vera! Come here! You should hear what they're doing down there in town, the bastards!"

Vera came back carrying a tray with a steaming bowl of soup. She sat down and Jakub had to resume the story of his adventure of the day before. The dog sat under the table, letting himself be scratched behind the ears.

When Jakub had finished his soup, the man got up and rushed off to the kitchen to bring back a dish of roast pork with dumplings.

Jakub was sitting by the window and feeling good. The man cursed the people down there (Jakub was fascinated: the man considered his restaurant a lofty place, an Olympus, a point of retreat and loftiness), and the woman went off to lead a two-year-old boy in by the hand: "Say thank you to the gentleman," she said. "He brought back your Bob."

The toddler babbled some unintelligible words and emitted a little laugh for Jakub. It was sunny outside, and the yellowing foliage bent gently over the open window. There was not a sound. The inn was well above the world, and one could find peace there.

Although he did not like to procreate, Jakub liked children: "You have a good-looking little boy," he said.

"He's a bit strange," said the woman. "I don't know where he got that big beak."

Jakub recalled his friend's nose and said: "Doctor Skreta told me that he took care of you."

"You know the doctor?" the man asked cheerily.

"He's a friend of mine," said Jakub.

"We're very grateful to him," said the young mother, and Jakub thought that the child was probably one of the successes of Skreta's eugenic project.

"He's not a physician, he's a magician," the man said admiringly.

Jakub reflected that, in this place where the peace of Bethlehem reigned, these three were a *holy family*, with the child begotten not by a human father but by the god Skreta.

The toddler with the big nose again babbled unintelligibly, and the young father gazed at him lovingly. "I wonder," he said to his wife, "which of your distant ancestors had a big nose."

Jakub smiled. A curious question had just occurred

to him: Had Dr. Skreta also used a syringe to impregnate his own wife?

"Isn't that right?" the young father asked.

"Of course," said Jakub. "It's a great consolation to think that when we've long been in the grave our noses will still be strolling the earth."

They all laughed, and the idea that Skreta could be the toddler's father now seemed to Jakub to be a fanciful dream.

5

Frantisek took the money from the lady whose refrigerator he had just fixed. He left the house, got on his faithful motorcycle, and headed toward the other end of town to hand over the day's receipts at the office in charge of repair services for the whole district. A few minutes after two he was through for the day. He started the motorcycle again and rode toward the thermal building. At the parking lot he saw the white sedan. He parked the motorcycle next to the car and walked under the colonnades toward the Hall of the People, because he surmised the trumpeter might be there.

He was driven neither by audacity nor combativeness. He no longer wanted to make a scene. On the contrary, he was determined to control himself, to yield, to submit totally. He told himself that his love was so great that he could bear anything for its sake. Like the fairy-tale prince who endures all kinds of torments and sufferings for the sake of the princess, confronting dragons and crossing oceans, he was ready to accept fabulously excessive humiliations.

Why was he so humble? Why did he not turn instead to another young woman, one of those available in the small spa town in such alluring abundance?

Frantisek is younger than Ruzena, and thus, unfortunately for him, he is very young. When he is more mature he will find out that things are transient, and he will become aware that beyond one woman's horizon there opens up a horizon of yet more women. But Frantisek still knows nothing about time. He has been living since childhood in an enduring, unchanging world, living in a kind of immobile eternity, he still has the same father and the same mother, and Ruzena, who had made a man of him, is above him like the lid of the firmament, of the only possible firmament. He cannot imagine life without her.

The day before, he had docilely promised not to spy on her and simultaneously had sincerely decided not to bother her. He told himself he was interested only in the trumpeter, and trailing him would not really be a violation of his promise. But at the same time he realized that this was only an excuse and that Ruzena would condemn his behavior, but it was stronger in him than any reflection or any resolution, it was like a drug addiction: he had to see the man; he had to see him once more, for a long time and close up. He had to look his torment in the face. He had to look at that body, whose union with Ruzena's body seemed to him unimaginable and unbelievable. He had to look at him to confirm with his own eyes whether it was possible to think of their two bodies united.

On the bandstand they were already playing: Dr. Skreta on drums, a slender man on piano, and Klima on trumpet. Some young jazz fans who had slipped in to listen to the rehearsal were sitting in the hall. Frantisek had no fear that the motive for his presence would be found out. He was certain that the trumpeter, blinded by the motorcycle's light, had not seen his face on Tuesday evening, and thanks to Ruzena's caution no one knew much about his relations with the young woman.

The trumpeter interrupted the musicians and sat down at the piano to show the slender man the right tempo. Frantisek took a seat in the back of the hall, slowly transforming himself into a shadow that would not for a moment leave the trumpeter that day.

6

He was driving back from the forest inn and regretted no longer having beside him the jolly dog who had licked his face. Then he thought it a miracle that he had succeeded for the forty-five years of his life in keeping that seat beside him free, enabling him now to leave the country so easily, with no baggage, with no burdens, alone, with a false (and yet beautiful) sensation of youth, as if he were a student just beginning to lay the foundation of his future.

He tried to get firmly in mind the idea that he was leaving his country. He tried hard to evoke his past life. He tried hard to see it as a landscape he looked back on with longing, a landscape vertiginously distant. But he could not manage it. What he did succeed in seeing behind him in his mind's eye was tiny, compressed like a closed accordion. He had to make an effort to evoke the scraps of memory that could give him the illusion of a destiny that had been lived.

He looked at the trees along the road. Their foliage was green, red, yellow, and brown. The forest looked aflame. He thought that he was departing at a moment when the forests were on fire and his life and memories were being consumed in those glorious and unfeeling flames. Should he hurt for not hurting? Should he be sad for not being sad?

He felt no sadness, but neither was he in any hurry. According to his arrangements with his friends abroad, he should already have crossed the border by now, but he felt he was again prey to that indecisive lethargy so well known and so much derided in his circle because he succumbed to it exactly when circumstances demanded energetic and resolute behavior. He knew that he was going to maintain to the last moment that he was leaving today, but he was also aware that since the morning he had done all he could to delay the moment of departure from this charming spa town where for years he had been coming to see his friend, sometimes after long intervals but always with pleasure.

He parked the car (yes, the trumpeter's white sedan and Frantisek's motorcycle were already there) and went into the brasserie, where Olga would be joining him in half an hour. He saw a table he liked, next to the bay window in back looking out at the park's flaming trees, but unfortunately it was already occupied by a man in his thirties. Jakub sat down nearby. He could not see the trees from there; he was fascinated instead by the man, who was visibly nervous, never taking his eyes off the door as he tapped his foot.

7

She finally arrived. Klima sprang up from his chair, went forward to meet her, and led her to the window table. He smiled at her as if trying by that smile to show that their agreement was still valid, that they were calm and in alliance, and that they had confidence in each other. He searched the young woman's expression for a positive response to his smile, but he didn't find it. That alarmed him. He didn't dare talk about what preoccupied him, and he engaged the young woman in a meaningless conversation that ought to have created a carefree atmosphere. Nonetheless his words echoed off the young woman's silence as though off a stone wall.

Then she interrupted him: "I've changed my mind. It would be a crime. You might be capable of something like that, but not me."

The trumpeter felt everything in him collapse. He fixed an expressionless look on Ruzena and no longer knew what to say. There was nothing in him but hopeless fatigue. And Ruzena repeated: "It would be a crime."

He looked at her, and she seemed unreal to him. This woman, whose face he was unable to recall when he was away from her, now presented herself to him as his life sentence. (Like all of us, Klima considered reality to be only what entered his life from inside, gradually and organically, whereas what came from outside, suddenly and randomly, he perceived as an invasion of unreality. Alas, nothing is more real than that unreality.)

Then the waiter who had recognized the trumpeter two days before appeared at their table. He brought them a tray with two brandies, and said jovially: "You see, I can read your wishes in your eyes." And to Ruzena he made the same remark as the last time: "Watch out! All the girls want to scratch your eyes out!" And he laughed very loudly.

This time Klima was too absorbed in his fear to pay attention to the waiter's words. He drank a mouthful of brandy and leaned toward Ruzena: "What's going on? I thought we agreed. It was all settled between us. Why did you suddenly change your mind? Just like me, you think we need a few years to devote ourselves entirely to each other. Ruzena! We're doing it only because of our love and to have a child together when both of us really want one."

8

Jakub instantly recognized the nurse who had wanted to turn Bob over to the old men. He looked at her, fascinated, very curious to know what she and the man with her were talking about. He could not distinguish a single word, but he saw clearly that the conversation was extremely fraught.

From the man's expression it soon became obvious that he had just heard distressing news. He needed a while to find his tongue. His gestures showed that he was trying to persuade the young woman, that he was imploring her. But the young woman remained obstinately silent.

Jakub could not keep from thinking that a life was at stake. The blonde young woman still seemed to him like someone ready to restrain the victim during an execution, and he didn't for a moment doubt that the man was on the side of life and that she was on the side of death. The man wanted to save someone's life, he was asking for help, but the blonde was refusing it and because of her someone was going to die.

And then he noticed that the man had stopped insisting, that he was smiling and was not hesitating to caress the young woman's cheek. Had they reached an agreement? Not at all. Under the yellow hair the face looked obstinately into the distance, avoiding the man's look.

Jakub was powerless to tear his eyes away from the young woman, whom he was unable since the day before to imagine other than as a hangman's assistant. She had a pretty and vacant face. Pretty enough to attract a man and vacant enough to make all his pleas vanish in it. That face was proud and, Jakub knew, proud not of its prettiness but of its vacuity.

He thought that he saw in that face thousands of other faces he knew well. He thought that his entire life had been an unbroken dialogue with that face. Whenever he had tried to explain something to it, that face had turned away, offended, responding to his arguments by talking about something else; whenever he had smiled at it, that face had reproached him for his superficiality; whenever he had implored it to do something, that face had accused him of exhibiting his superiority—that face which understood nothing and decided everything, a face as vacant as a desert and proud of its desertedness.

It occurred to him that today he was looking at that face for the last time, that tomorrow he was leaving its realm.

9

Ruzena too had noticed Jakub and recognized him. She felt his eyes fixed on her, and it made her nervous. She found herself surrounded by two men in tacit collusion, surrounded by two gazes pointed at her like two gun barrels.

Klima kept going over his arguments, and she didn't know how to reply. She preferred to repeat quickly to herself that when it was a matter of the life of a child-to-be, reason had nothing to say and only feelings had the right to speak. In silence she turned her face out of range of the double gaze and looked fixedly out the window. Then, thanks to a certain degree of concentration, she felt beginning in her the offended consciousness of a misunderstood lover and mother, and this consciousness was rising in her soul like dumpling dough. And because she was unable to express this feeling in words, she let it be conveyed by fixing her eyes on a single spot in the park.

But precisely where her dazed eyes were fixed she suddenly saw a familiar figure and was panic-stricken.

She no longer heard what Klima was saying. Now there was a third gaze pointing its gun barrel at her, and it was the most dangerous. For Ruzena had been unable to tell with certainty who was responsible for her pregnancy. The one she had thought of first was the man now watching her on the sly, poorly hidden by a tree. But that was only obvious at the beginning, for as time passed she more and more favored choosing the trumpeter as begetter, until the day when she finally decided that it was most certainly he. Let us be utterly clear: she was not trying to attribute her pregnancy to him through trickery. In making her decision, she chose not trickery but truth. She decided it was *truly* so.

Besides, pregnancy is such a sacred thing that it seemed to her impossible that a man she so looked down on could be the cause of it. It was not logical reasoning but a kind of suprarational illumination that had convinced her she could only have become pregnant by a man she liked, respected, and admired. And when she heard over the telephone that the one she had chosen as the father of her child was shocked, frightened, and refusing to accept his paternal mission, everything was settled conclusively, for from that moment on, not only did she no longer doubt her truth, but she was ready to fight for it.

Klima was silent, and he caressed Ruzena's cheek. Brought out of her reflections, she noticed that he was smiling. He said that they should take another ride in the country, for this brasserie table was separating them like a wall.

She was afraid. Frantisek was still behind the tree in the park with his eyes fixed on the brasserie window. What would happen if he were to harass them as they were leaving? What would happen if he were to make a scene, as he had on Tuesday?

"I'll pay for the two brandies now," Klima said to the waiter.

Ruzena took a glass tube out of her handbag.

The trumpeter gave the waiter a bill and with a magnanimous gesture refused the change.

Ruzena opened the tube, shook a tablet into the hollow of her hand, and swallowed it.

When she closed the tube again, the trumpeter turned to her and looked her in the face. He moved both his hands toward hers, and she let go of the tube in order to feel the touch of his fingers.

"Come, let's go," he said, and Ruzena got up. She saw Jakub's gaze, fixed and hostile, and she looked away.

Once they were outside, she looked anxiously toward the park, but Frantisek was no longer there.

10

Jakub got up and, taking his half-full glass with him, sat down at the vacated table. With satisfaction he cast a glance through the window at the reddening trees in the park, and again he thought that these trees were like a fire into which he was throwing his forty-five years of life. Then his glance slipped to the surface of the table, and next to the ashtray he saw the forgotten glass tube. He picked it up and examined it: on the label was the name of a drug unfamiliar to him, with a penciled addition: "Three times a day." The tablets inside the tube were pale blue. That seemed odd to him.

These were the last hours he was spending in his country, and the smallest events were being charged with extraordinary meaning and being changed into an allegorical show. What does it mean, he asked himself, that on this very day someone has left on a table for me a tube of pale-blue tablets? And why should it have been left here by that very woman, Political Persecution's Heiress and Hangman's Assistant? Was she trying to tell me that the need for pale-blue tablets was not yet over? Or was she really trying, by this allusion to poison tablets, to express her undying hatred? Or, still more, was she trying to tell me that by leaving the country I am showing the same resignation I would be showing if I were to swallow the pale-blue tablet I carry in my jacket pocket?

He searched in his pocket, pulled out the tiny wad of tissue paper, and unfolded it. Now that he was looking at it, his own tablet seemed to him a shade darker than those in the forgotten tube. He opened the tube and shook a tablet into his hand. Yes, his was a bit darker and smaller. One after the other, he put the two tablets into the glass tube. Now that he was looking at them together, he saw that at first sight one would be unable to tell the difference. On top, above the harmless tablets probably intended to treat the mildest of ailments, death lay concealed.

At that moment Olga approached the table. Jakub quickly capped the tube, put it next to the ashtray, and rose to greet his friend.

"I just ran into Klima, the famous trumpeter! Is that possible?" she asked, sitting down beside Jakub. "He was with that horrible female! She gave me a hard time today at the baths!"

But she broke off, for at that moment Ruzena planted herself at their table and said: "I left my tablets here."

Before Jakub could reply, she noticed the tube next to the ashtray and reached for it.

But Jakub was quicker and grabbed it first.

"Give me that!" said Ruzena.

"I want to ask you a favor," said Jakub. "May I have one of those tablets?"

"Sorry! I haven't got time!"

"I'm taking the same drug, and . . ."

"I'm not a walking pharmacy," said Ruzena.

Jakub tried to remove the cap, but Ruzena prevented him by abruptly reaching for it. Jakub instantly grasped the tube in his fist.

"What's this all about? Give me those tablets!" the young woman shouted at him.

Jakub looked her in the eye; slowly he opened his hand.

11

Over the rhythmic clatter of the wheels, the futility of her trip seemed clear. She was sure at any rate that her husband was not in the spa town. Then why was she going there? Was she taking a four-hour train trip only to find out what she already knew? She was not acting on a rational intention. It was an engine within her, which had taken to turning and turning and which there was no way of stopping.

(Yes, at this moment Frantisek and Kamila are being propelled into the space of the story like two rockets guided from a distance by blind jealousy—but what guidance can blindness provide?)

Rail connections between the capital and the spa town were not the simplest, and Mrs. Klima had to change trains three times before she got off, exhausted, at an idyllic station filled with display advertisements recommending the locality's healing springs and miraculous muds. She took the poplar-lined avenue that led from the station to the thermal baths, and, arriving at the colonnades, she was struck by a hand-painted poster on which her husband's name appeared in red. Surprised, she stopped and under her husband's name read two other men's names. She couldn't believe it: Klima hadn't lied to her! It was exactly what he had told her. In these first few seconds she experienced great joy, feeling again the trust she had lost long ago.

But her joy didn't last long, for she immediately realized that the existence of the concert was no proof of her husband's fidelity. He certainly must have agreed to perform in this isolated spa town in order to revisit a woman. And suddenly she became aware that the situation was actually worse than she had imagined, that she had fallen into a trap:

She had come here to make sure that her husband was elsewhere, and thus *indirectly* to prove him guilty (yet again, for the umpteenth time!) of infidelity. But now things had changed: She was not going to catch him in a blatant lie but catch him (*directly*, with her own eyes) in an act of infidelity. Whether she wanted to or not, she was going to see the woman with whom Klima had spent the day. This thought nearly staggered her. Of course she had long been certain that she *knew* everything, but until now she had never *seen* anything (any of his mistresses). To tell the truth, she knew nothing at all, she only believed she knew, and she gave this conjecture the weight of certainty. She believed in her husband's infidelity the way a Christian believes in God's existence. But the Christian believes in God with the absolute certainty that He will remain unseen. The thought that today she was going to see Klima with a woman made her feel the terror a Christian would feel on receiving a phone call from God announcing that He was coming over for lunch.

Her entire body was overwhelmed by anxiety. Then she heard someone call her name. She turned around and saw three young men standing under the colonnades. They wore sweaters and jeans, and their bohemian style contrasted sharply with the dreary tidiness of the other spa clientele strolling by. They greeted her with laughter.

"What a surprise!" she exclaimed. They were film people, friends from her days onstage with a microphone.

The tallest one, a director, quickly took her by the arm: "How pleasant it would be to know that you came because of us . . ."

"But you came here because of your husband . . ." the assistant director said sadly.

"Just our lousy luck!" said the director. "The most beautiful woman in the capital, and that lout of a trumpeter keeps her in a cage so you don't get to see her for years."

"Shit!" said the cameraman (the short young man in the torn sweater), "we have to celebrate this!"

They thought they were devoting their effusive admiration to a radiant queen who was absentmindedly hastening to throw it into a wicker basket filled with disdained gifts. And Kamila meanwhile was receiving their words with the gratitude of a lame girl leaning on a kindly arm.

12

While Olga talked, Jakub was thinking that he had just given poison to a stranger, a young woman who was in danger of swallowing it at any moment.

It had happened suddenly, happened so quickly that he had not even had time to become aware of it. It had happened without his knowledge.

Olga kept talking, and Jakub was searching his mind for justification, telling himself that he had not wanted to give the young woman the tube, that she and she alone had forced him to do it.

But he quickly realized that this was a glib excuse. There were a thousand possible ways he could have disobeyed her. He could have opposed the young woman's insolence with his own insolence, could calmly have shaken the first tablet into the hollow of his hand and put it in his pocket.

And since he had lacked the presence of mind to do this, he could have rushed after the young woman and confessed that there was poison in the tube. It was not too hard to explain to her how it had happened.

But rather than do anything, he remains sitting in his chair and looking at Olga while she is telling him something. He should be getting up, running to catch the nurse. There is still time. And it is his duty to do everything he can to save her life. Why then is he sitting in his chair, why doesn't he move?

Olga was talking, and he was amazed that he stayed sitting, immobile in his chair.

He decided that he must get up right now and look for the nurse. He wondered how he was going to explain to Olga that he must leave. Should he confess to her what had happened? He concluded that he could not confess it to her. What if the nurse swallowed the tablet before he could get to her? Should Olga know that Jakub was a murderer? And even if he got to the nurse in time, how could he justify his long hesitation to Olga and make her understand it? How could he explain to her why he had given the woman the tube? From now on, because of these moments of doing nothing, of remaining rooted to his chair, any observer would have to see him as a murderer!

No, he could not confess to Olga, but what could he say to her? How could he explain abruptly getting up and running God knows where?

But what did it matter what he might say to her? How could he still be occupying himself with such foolishness? How could he, when it was a matter of life and death, care about what Olga was going to think?

He knew that his reflections were quite uncalled for and that every second of hesitation increased the danger threatening the nurse. Actually, it was already too late. While he had been hesitating, she and her friend had already gotten so far from the brasserie that Jakub would not even know in what direction to look for her. If only he knew where they had gone! Where could he find them?

But he soon reproached himself that this argument was just another excuse. It would certainly be hard to find them quickly, but it was not impossible. It was not too late to act, but he had to act immediately, or else it would be too late!

"I started the day badly," Olga was saying. "I overslept, I was late for breakfast and they refused to serve me any, and at the baths there were those stupid film people. To think that I was longing so to have a beautiful day, since it's the last one I'll be spending here with you. It's so important to me. Do you have any idea, Jakub, how important it is to me?"

She leaned across the table and grasped his hands.

"Don't worry, there's no reason for you to spend a bad day," he said with an effort, for he was unable to fix his attention on her. A voice was constantly reminding him that the nurse had poison in her handbag and that her life and death depended on him. It was an intrusive, insistent voice, but at the same time strangely weak, as if it were coming to him from far too distant depths.

13

Klima was driving with Ruzena along a forest road, noting that this time a ride in his luxurious sedan would not at all be working in his favor. Nothing could distract Ruzena from her stubborn silence, and the trumpeter himself stopped talking for quite a while. When the silence had become too heavy, he said: "Are you coming to the concert?"

"I don't know," she answered.

"Please come," he said, and that evening's concert provided the pretext for a conversation that momentarily diverted them from their quarrel. Klima made an effort to speak amusingly about the drum-playing physician, and decided to postpone the conclusive encounter with Ruzena until the evening.

"I hope you'll be waiting for me after the concert," he said. "Like the last time I played here." As soon as he said these words he realized their significance. "Like the last time" meant that they would make love after the concert. My God, why hadn't he considered that possibility?

It was odd, but until that moment the idea that he might go to bed with her had never even crossed his mind. Ruzena's pregnancy had gently and imperceptibly pushed her away into the asexual terrain of anxiety. Of course he had urged himself to show tenderness toward her, to kiss and caress her, and he made a point of doing so, but these were only gestures, empty signs, without any corporeal interest.

Reflecting on it now, he realized that this indifference to Ruzena's body was the most serious mistake he had made in the last few days. Yes, it was now absolutely clear to him (and he was indignant that the friends he had consulted had not brought it to his attention): he absolutely had to go to bed with her! Because the remoteness the young woman had suddenly assumed, and he was unable to break through, came precisely from the continuing estrangement of their bodies. Rejecting the child, the flower of Ruzena's womb, was at the same time a wounding rejection of her gravid body. He thus had to show all the more interest in her nongravid body. He had to oppose the fertile body with the infertile body as his ally.

This analysis gave him a feeling of renewed hope. He put his arm around Ruzena's shoulder and leaned toward her: "It breaks my heart to think of us quarreling. Listen, we'll definitely find a solution. The main thing is that we'll be together. We won't let anybody deprive us of tonight, and it'll be as beautiful a night as last time."

One arm held the wheel, the other was around Ruzena's shoulders, and all of a sudden he thought he felt, deep down, a rising desire for the naked skin of this young woman, and this delighted him, for desire was in position to provide him with the only language he and she spoke in common.

"And where'll we meet?" she asked.

Klima was aware that the whole spa town would see with whom he was leaving the concert. But there was no getting around it: "As soon as I'm finished, come and get me behind the bandstand."

14

While Klima was hurrying back to the Hall of the People to rehearse "St. Louis Blues" and "When the Saints Go Marching In" one last time, Ruzena was looking around anxiously. Not long before, in the car, she had observed in the rearview mirror several times that Frantisek was following them at a distance on his motorcycle. But now he was nowhere to be seen.

She felt she was a fugitive pursued by time. She realized that by tomorrow she would have to know what she wanted, and she knew nothing. In the whole world there was not one person she trusted. Her own family was alien to her. Frantisek loved her, but that was just why she mistrusted him (as the doe mistrusts the hunter). She mistrusted Klima (as the hunter mistrusts the doe). She liked her colleagues well enough, but she did not quite trust them (as the hunter mistrusts other hunters). She was alone in life, and for the past few weeks she had been carrying in her womb a strange companion who some maintained was her greatest chance and others completely the opposite, a companion toward whom she herself felt only indifference.

She knew nothing. She was filled to the brim with not knowing. She was nothing but not knowing. She didn't even know where she was going.

She was passing the Slavia, the worst restaurant in the spa town, a filthy café where the locals came to drink beer and spit on the floor. In the old days it had probably been the best, and from those times there still remained a small garden with three red wooden tables and their chairs (paint peeling), a memento of bourgeois pleasure in open-air brass bands and dancing and parasols propped against the chairs. But what did she know about those times, this young woman who merely went through life on the narrow footbridge of the present, devoid of all historical memory? She was unable to see the shadow the pink parasol casts on us from a distant time, she only saw three young men in jeans, a beautiful woman, and a bottle of wine standing in the middle of a bare table.

One of the men called out to her. She turned and recognized the short cameraman in the torn sweater.

"Come have a drink with us!" he exclaimed.

She complied.

"Thanks to this charming young lady we were able to shoot a little porn film this morning," said the cameraman, by way of introducing Ruzena to the woman, who offered her hand and unintelligibly murmured her name.

Ruzena sat down beside the cameraman, who put a glass in front of her and filled it with wine.

Ruzena was grateful that something was happening. That she no longer had to wonder where she was going or what she should do. That she no longer had to decide whether or not to keep the child.

15

He had finally made up his mind. He paid the waiter and told Olga that he had to leave and that they would meet before the concert.

Olga asked him what it was he had to do, and Jakub had the unpleasant sensation of being interrogated. He answered that he had an appointment with Skreta.

"All right," she said, "but that won't take you very long. I'll go and change, and I'll be here at six. I'm inviting you to dinner."

Jakub accompanied Olga to Karl Marx House. When she had disappeared down the corridor, he turned to the doorkeeper: "Would you tell me, please, if Miss Ruzena is in?"

"No," said the doorkeeper. "The key's hanging on the board."

"I have something extremely urgent to tell her," said Jakub. "Do you know where I might find her?"

"I don't know."

"I saw her a while ago with the trumpeter who's giving a concert this evening."

"Yes, me too I hear tell she's going out with him," said the doorkeeper. "Right now he must be rehearsing in the Hall of the People."

When Dr. Skreta, enthroned on the bandstand behind his set of drums, caught sight of Jakub in the doorway, he nodded to him. Jakub smiled at him and examined the rows of seats in which about a dozen fans were sitting. (Yes, Frantisek, Klima's shadow, was among them.) Then Jakub sat down, hoping that the nurse would finally appear.

He wondered where he might still go looking for her. At this moment she might be in any number of different places he had no idea of. Should he ask the trumpeter? But how would he pose the question? And what if something had already happened to Ruzena? Jakub had already concluded that if she died, her death would be totally inexplicable, that a murderer who killed without a motive could not be caught. Should he attract attention to himself? Did he have to leave a trail and lay himself open to suspicion?

He called himself to order. A human life was in danger, and he had no right to be thinking in such a cowardly way. He took advantage of a pause between two numbers and climbed up on the back of the bandstand. Skreta turned toward him, beaming, but Jakub put a finger to his lips and begged him in an undertone to ask the trumpeter the whereabouts of the nurse he had noticed him with an hour earlier in the brasserie.

"What do all of you see in her?" Skreta grumbled sullenly. "Where's Ruzena?" he then cried out to the trumpeter, who blushed and said he didn't know.

"Never mind!" said Jakub apologetically. "Go on playing!"

"How do you like our band?" asked Dr. Skreta.

"It's great," said Jakub, and he climbed down and returned to his seat. He knew that he was still behaving wrongly. If he really cared about Ruzena's life, he would move heaven and earth to alert everyone to find her immediately. But he had set out to look for her only so as to have an alibi to present to his own conscience.

Again he recalled the moment when he had given her the tube containing the poison. Had it really happened so quickly that he had not had the time to be aware of it? Had it really happened without his knowledge?

Jakub knew that this was not true. His conscience had not been lulled. He again evoked the face under the blonde hair, and he realized it was not by accident (not by lulling his conscience) that he had given the nurse the tube containing the poison, but that it was an old desire of his which for years had watched for the opportunity, a desire so powerful that the opportunity finally obeyed it and came rushing toward it.

He shuddered and got up from his seat. He ran off to Karl Marx House, but Ruzena was still not home.

16

What an idyll, what a respite! What an interlude in the middle of the drama! What a voluptuous afternoon with three fauns!

The trumpeter's two persecutors, his two hardships, are seated opposite each other, both drinking wine from the same bottle and both equally happy to be where they are, able if only for a while to do something other than think about him. What a touching alliance, what harmony!

Mrs. Klima looks at the three men. She had once been part of their circle, and she looks at them now as if at a negative of her present life. Submerged by cares, she is seated here facing pure carefreeness; bound to one man, she is seated here facing three fauns who embody virility in its infinite variety.

The fauns' remarks have an obvious goal: to spend the night with the two women, spend the night in a fivesome. It is an illusory goal, because they know that Mrs. Klima's husband is here, but the goal is so beautiful that they are pursuing it even though it is unreachable.

Mrs. Klima knows what they are getting at, and she abandons herself all the more easily to the pursuit of this goal that is merely a fantasy, merely a game, merely a dream temptation. She laughs at their ambiguous remarks, she trades encouraging jokes with the nameless woman who is her accomplice, and she hopes to prolong the drama's interlude as long as possible in order to delay still longer the moment when she will see her rival and look truth in the face.

Yet another bottle of wine, everyone is cheerful, everyone is a bit drunk, but less on wine than on the oddness of the atmosphere, on that desire to prolong the very rapidly passing moment.

Mrs. Klima feels the director's calf pressing her left leg under the table. She is well aware of it, but she does not withdraw her leg. It is a contact that establishes a sensual connection between them, but it could also have happened quite by chance, could very well have gone unnoticed by her because of its triviality. It is thus a contact situated right on the border between innocence and shamelessness. Kamila does not want to cross this border, but she is happy to be able to stay on it (on this thin sliver of unexpected freedom), and she would be still happier if this magic line were to shift itself toward other verbal allusions, other touchings, other games. Protected by the innocent ambiguity of this shifting border, she wishes to let herself be carried far away, far away and still farther.

Whereas Kamila's beauty, radiant to the point of being nearly embarrassing, forces the director to conduct his offensive with cautious slowness, Ruzena's ordinary charm attracts the cameraman powerfully and directly. He has his arm around her and his hand on her breast.

Kamila is watching. It has been a long time since she has seen up close the shameless gestures of others! She looks at the man's hand covering the young woman's breast, kneading it, pressing and caressing it through her clothing. She is watching Ruzena's face, immobile, passive, tinged with sensual abandon. The hand is caressing the breast, time is sweetly passing, and Kamila feels the assistant's knee against her other leg.

And now she says: "I'm really going to live it up tonight."

"To hell with your trumpeter husband!" the director retorts.

"Yes, to hell with him!" the assistant repeats.

17

At that moment Ruzena recognized her. Yes, that was the face in the photograph her colleague had shown her! She suddenly pushed away the cameraman's hand.

"You're crazy!" he complained.

He tried to put his arm around her again, and again he was pushed away.

"How dare you!" she shouted at him.

The director and his assistant laughed. "Do you really mean it?" the assistant asked Ruzena.

"Sure I mean it," she answered sternly.

The assistant looked at his watch and said to the cameraman: "It's exactly six o'clock. This complete reversal is taking place because our friend becomes a virtuous woman every even-numbered hour. So you have to wait until seven o'clock."

The laughter burst out again. Ruzena was red with humiliation. She had let herself be caught with a stranger's hand on her breast. She had let herself be caught being pawed. She had let herself be caught by her greatest rival while everyone was making fun of her.

The director said to the cameraman: "Maybe you should request the young lady to make an exception and consider six an odd-numbered hour."

"Do you think it's theoretically possible to consider six an odd number?" asked the assistant.

"Yes," said the director. "In his famous *Elements*, Euclid literally says so: 'In certain particular and very mysterious circumstances, certain even numbers behave like odd numbers.' It seems to me that we're dealing with mysterious circumstances of that kind right now."

"Do you, Ruzena, therefore agree to consider six o'clock an odd-numbered hour?" said the assistant.

Ruzena remained silent.

"Do you agree?" asked the cameraman, leaning toward her.

"The young lady is silent," said the assistant. "It's therefore up to us to decide if we should take her silence as consent or as refusal."

"We can vote," said the director.

"That's fair," said the assistant. "Who is in favor of the proposition that Ruzena agrees in this case that six is an odd number? Kamila! You vote first!"

"I think that Ruzena absolutely agrees," said Kamila.

"And you, Director?"

"I'm convinced," said the director in his gentle voice, "that Miss Ruzena will agree to consider six an odd number."

"The cameraman is too much of an interested party, and so he can't vote. As for me, I vote in favor," said the assistant. "We've therefore decided, three votes to none, that Ruzena's silence is equivalent to consent. From this it follows, cameraman, that you may immediately resume pursuing your advances."

The cameraman leaned toward Ruzena and put his arm around her so that his hand was once more touching her breast. Ruzena pushed him away even more violently than before and shouted: "Get your filthy paws off me!"

Kamila interceded: "Look, Ruzena, he can't help it that he likes you so much. We've all been having such a good time . . ."

A few minutes earlier Ruzena had been quite passive and had given herself up to the course of events to do with her what it wished, as if she hoped to read her fate in whatever chance brought her way. She would have let herself be taken away, she would have let herself be seduced and persuaded of anything, just to escape from the dead end in which she found herself trapped.

But chance, to which she lifted her imploring face, suddenly proved to be hostile, and Ruzena, held up to ridicule in front of her rival and made into a laughing-stock, realized that she had only one single solid support, one single consolation, one single chance of salvation: the embryo in her womb. Her entire soul went down (once more! once more!), down inside to the inmost depths of her body, and Ruzena became more and more convinced that she would never part with him who was quietly burgeoning within her. In him she held a secret trump card that lifted her high above their laughter and their unclean hands. She had an intense craving to tell them, to shout it in their faces, to take revenge on them for their sarcasm, to take revenge on that woman and her patronizing kindliness.

Keep calm! she told herself, and she rummaged in her handbag for the tube. She had just pulled it out when she felt a hand firmly gripping her wrist.

18

No one had seen him coming. He had appeared all of a sudden, and Ruzena looked up and saw him smile.

He kept restraining her hand; Ruzena felt the strong touch of his fingers on her wrist, and she obeyed: the tube dropped back into the bottom of the handbag.

"Please allow me, ladies and gentlemen, to sit down at your table. My name is Bertlef."

None of the men was enthusiastic about the intruder's arrival, none of them introduced himself, and Ruzena did not have enough social grace to introduce her companions to him.

"My unexpected arrival seems to have disconcerted

you," said Bertlef. He took a chair from a nearby table and put it at the vacant end of their table and sat down, so that he was presiding and had Ruzena at his right. "Forgive me," he went on. "For a long time I have had the peculiar habit of not arriving but appearing."

"In that case," said the assistant, "allow us to treat you as an apparition and pay no attention to you."

"I gladly allow you that," said Bertlef with a slight bow. "But I am afraid that despite my willingness you will not succeed."

Then he turned to look at the doorway to the Slavia's brightly lit indoor restaurant and clapped his hands.

"Who invited you here, Chief?" asked the cameraman.

"Are you trying to tell me that I am not welcome? I could leave right now with Ruzena, but a habit is a habit. I come to this table every day in the late afternoon to drink a bottle of wine." He examined the label of the bottle standing on the table: "But certainly a better wine than the one you are drinking."

"I wonder where you find any good wine in this dump," said the assistant.

"My impression, Chief, is that you brag too much," the cameraman added, seeking to ridicule the intruder. "It's true that after a certain age one can hardly do anything else."

"You are wrong," said Bertlef as if he had not heard the cameraman's insult, "they still have some bottles hidden here that are a great deal better than what you can find in the grandest hotels."

He was shaking the hand of the manager, who had been barely visible earlier but was now welcoming Bertlef and asking him: "Shall I set the table for everyone?"

"Certainly," Bertlef replied, and turned to the others: "Ladies and gentlemen, I invite you to drink a wine with me that I have had here a number of times and find excellent. Do you accept the invitation?"

No one replied to Bertlef, and the manager said: "When it's a matter of food and drink, I can advise the ladies and gentlemen to have full confidence in Mister Bertlef."

"My friend," Bertlef said to the manager, "bring two bottles and a platter of cheese." Then, turning to the others: "Your hesitation is unnecessary, Ruzena's friends are friends of mine."

A boy of no more than twelve came running out of the restaurant carrying a tray with glasses, saucers, and a tablecloth. He put the tray on a nearby table and then leaned over the customers one by one to remove their half-full glasses. He parked these, along with the open bottle, next to the tray he had just put on the nearby table. Then he carefully wiped their visibly dirty table with a dish towel and spread on it a tablecloth of dazzling whiteness. After that he went back to the nearby table to get the glasses and put them back in front of the customers.

"Get rid of those glasses and that bottle of vinegar," Bertlef said to the boy. "Your papa will bring us better wine."

The cameraman protested: "Would you be kind enough, Chief, to let us drink what we like?"

"As you wish, sir," said Bertlef. "I am not in favor of imposing happiness on people. Everyone has a right to his bad wine, to his stupidity, and to his dirty fingernails. Listen, son," he said, turning to the boy: "Give each of them back the old glass and an empty new one. My guests can choose freely between a wine produced in fog and a wine born of the sun."

So now there were two glasses per person, one empty and the other with leftover wine. The manager approached the table with two bottles, gripped one between his knees, and pulled out the cork with a grandiose gesture. Then he poured a bit of wine into Bertlef's glass. Bertlef brought his glass to his lips, took a sip, and turned to the manager: "Excellent. Is it the twenty-three?"

"It's the twenty-two," the manager corrected.

"Pour it!" said Bertlef, and the manager went around the table with the bottle and filled the empty glasses.

Bertlef held up his glass by the stem. "My friends, taste this wine. It has the sweet taste of the past. Savor it as if you were breathing it in, sucking in a long boneful of marrow, a long-forgotten summer. I would like with this toast to marry the past and the present, the sun of nineteen twenty-two and the sun of this moment. That sun is Ruzena, that thoroughly simple young woman who is a queen without knowing it. Against the backdrop of this spa town, she is like a diamond on a mendicant's robe. She is like a crescent moon forgotten against the pale sky of day. She is like a butterfly fluttering against the snow."

The cameraman gave a forced laugh: "Aren't you overdoing it, Chief?"

"No, I am not overdoing it," said Bertlef, and then he addressed the cameraman: "You are under that impression because you merely live in the basement of being, you anthropomorphized barrel of vinegar! You are filled with acids seething in you as in an alchemist's pot! You are devoting your life to discovering around you the same ugliness you carry within you. That is the only way you can feel at peace for a moment with the world. Because the world, which is beautiful, frightens you, sickens you, and constantly pushes you away from its center. How unbearable it is to have dirt under your fingernails and a pretty woman sitting beside you! And so you have to soil the woman before you enjoy her. Isn't it so, sir? I am glad you are hiding your hands under the table, I was certainly right to have talked about your fingernails."

"I don't give a shit about your good manners, and I'm not a clown like you with your white collar and tie," the cameraman snapped.

"Your dirty fingernails and torn sweater are not new under the sun," said Bertlef. "Long ago one of the Cynic philosophers strutted through the streets of Athens in a torn mantle to make himself admired by everyone for displaying his contempt for convention. One day Socrates met him and said: 'I see your vanity through the hole in your mantle.' Your dirt too, sir, is vanity, and your vanity is dirty."

Ruzena could not get over her amazement. A man she had vaguely known as a patient had come to her aid out of the blue, and she was captivated by the natural charm of his behavior and by the cruel assurance with which he had reduced the cameraman's insolence to dust.

"I see that you have lost the power of speech," Bertlef said to the cameraman after a brief silence, "and please believe that I did not in the least wish to offend you. I love harmony, not quarrels, and if I allowed myself to be carried away by eloquence, I ask you to forgive me. I want only one thing, that you taste this wine and join me in toasting Ruzena, for whose sake I have come here."

Bertlef had raised his glass, but no one joined him.

"Mister Restaurateur," said Bertlef, addressing the manager, "come and drink a toast with us!"

"With this wine, any time," said the manager, and he took an empty glass from the nearby table and filled it with wine. "Mister Bertlef knows all about good wine. A long time ago he sniffed out my cellar like a swallow finding its nest from a distance."

Bertlef emitted the happy laugh of a man whose self-esteem has been flattered.

"Will you join us in a toast to Ruzena?"

"Ruzena?" asked the manager.

"Yes, Ruzena," Bertlef said, indicating his neighbor with a look. "Do you like her as much as I do?"

"With you, Mister Bertlef, there're only pretty women. You barely have to look at her to know she's beautiful, since she's sitting next to you."

Bertlef once more emitted his happy laugh, the manager laughed with him, and oddly enough, Kamila, who had found Bertlef amusing ever since his arrival, joined them. This unexpected laughter was surprisingly and inexplicably contagious. Out of tactful solidarity the director in turn joined Kamila, then the assistant, and finally Ruzena, who plunged into the polyphonic laughter as if into a gentle embrace. It was her first laughter of the day. She laughed louder than the others and was unable to get her fill of it.

Bertlef lifted his raised glass higher: "To Ruzena!" The manager raised his glass in turn, and then Kamila, followed by the director and his assistant, and they repeated after Bertlef: "To Ruzena!" Even the cameraman ended up raising his glass and, without a word, taking a sip.

The director tasted his mouthful. "This wine really is excellent," he said.

"What did I tell you?" said the manager.

Meanwhile the boy had set a platter of cheese in the middle of the table, and Bertlef said: "Help yourselves, they are exquisite!"

The director was astounded: "Where did you find this selection of cheeses? You'd think we were in France."

All of a sudden the tension had completely receded, the atmosphere had calmed. They became talkative, helped themselves to the cheeses, wondered where the manager had managed to find them (in this country where the varieties of cheese were so few), and kept refilling their glasses.

When things were at their peak, Bertlef rose and took his leave: "I am very glad to have been in your company, and I thank you. My friend Doctor Skreta is giving a concert this evening, and Ruzena and I want to be there."

19

Ruzena and Bertlef vanished into the light mist of nightfall, and the initial momentum that had carried the company of drinkers away to the dreamed-of island of lustfulness had clearly been lost, and nothing could restore it. Everyone gave way to disheartenment.

For Mrs. Klima it was as if she were coming out of a dream in which she would have wished at all costs to linger. She had been reflecting that she didn't have to go to the concert. How fantastically surprising it would be for her to discover that she had come here not to track down her husband but to have an adventure. How splendid it would be to stay with the three film people and return home on the sly tomorrow morning.

Something whispered to her that this was what she needed to do; that this would be to act; to be delivered; to be healed; to be awakened after a bewitchment.

But now she was already too sober. All the magic spells had stopped working. She was alone again with herself, with her past, with her heavy head full of agonizing old thoughts. She would have liked to extend this much too brief dream, even if only for a few hours, but she knew that the dream was already growing pale, like the half light of early morning.

"I have to go too," she said.

They tried to dissuade her, even though they realized that they no longer had the power and self-confidence to make her stay.

"Shit!" said the cameraman. "Who was that guy, anyway?"

They tried to ask the manager, but now that Bertlef had left, once again no one was paying attention to them. From the restaurant came the noise of tipsy customers, while they sat abandoned around the table in the garden with their leftover cheese and wine.

"Whoever he is, he spoiled our party. He took away one of our ladies, and now the other one is going off all alone. Let's go with Kamila."

"No," she said. "Stay here. I wish to be alone."

She was no longer with them. Their presence now disturbed her. Jealousy, like death, had come looking for her. She was in its power, and she took no notice of anyone else. She got up and went off in the direction Bertlef and Ruzena had taken a few moments earlier.

From a distance she heard the cameraman saying: "Shit . . ."

20

After greeting Skreta in the artists' room, Jakub and Olga went into the hall. Olga wanted to leave during the intermission in order to spend the rest of the evening alone with Jakub. Jakub replied that his friend would be angered by their early departure, but Olga maintained that he wouldn't even notice it.

The hall was just about full, with only their two seats still vacant in their row.

"That woman has been following us like a shadow," said Olga, leaning toward Jakub as they sat down.

Jakub turned his head and next to Olga saw Bertlef and next to him the nurse with the poison in her handbag. His heart skipped a beat, but since he had tried hard all his life to hide what was going on deep down inside him, he said quite calmly: "I see that our row's tickets are the complimentary ones Skreta gave to his friends and acquaintances. So he knows where we are, and he'd notice us leaving."

"Tell him that the acoustics were bad here and that we moved to the back of the hall during intermission," said Olga.

Klima was already coming forward on the bandstand with his golden trumpet, and the audience began to applaud. When Dr. Skreta appeared behind him, the applause gained strength and murmuring swelled through the hall. Dr. Skreta stood modestly behind the trumpeter and awkwardly waved his arms to indicate that the concert's real star was the guest from the capital. The audience perceived the exquisite awkwardness of the gesture and reacted to it by applauding still louder. In back of the hall someone shouted: "Long live Doctor Skreta!"

The pianist, who was the most unobtrusive and least acclaimed of the three, sat down at the piano on a low chair. Skreta took his place behind an imposing set of drums, and the trumpeter came and went between the pianist and Skreta with a light and rhythmic step.

The applause ended, and the pianist struck the keyboard to begin a solo introduction. But Jakub noticed that his friend seemed nervous and was looking around in exasperation. Then the trumpeter, too, became aware of the physician's distress and approached him. Skreta whispered something to him. The two men bent over. They examined the floor, and then the trumpeter picked up a drumstick that had fallen at the foot of the piano and handed it to Skreta.

The audience, which had been watching the whole scene attentively, burst into new applause, and the pianist, thinking that the acclaim was in tribute to his solo, nodded his head in acknowledgment as he continued to play.

Olga took hold of Jakub's arm and whispered into his ear: "This is marvelous! So marvelous I think that from this moment on my lousy luck today is over."

The trumpet and drums finally joined in. Klima was blowing in time with his small rhythmic steps, and Skreta sat enthroned over his drums like a splendid, dignified Buddha.

Jakub imagined the nurse thinking of her medicine during the concert, swallowing the tablet, collapsing in convulsions, and slumping dead in her seat while on the bandstand Dr. Skreta banged his drums and the audience yelled and applauded.

And all of a sudden he understood clearly why the young woman was sitting in the same row as he: the unexpected encounter in the brasserie a while ago had been a temptation, a test. It had occurred only so that he might see his own image in the mirror: the image of a man who gives his neighbor poison. But the One who is testing him (God, in whom he does not believe) demands no bloody sacrifice, no blood of innocents. The test might end not in a death but only in Jakub's self-revelation, which might confiscate his inappropriate moral pride. The nurse is now sitting in the same row to enable him, at the last moment, to save her life. And that is also why she has next to her a man who the day before became Jakub's friend and who will help him.

Yes, he will wait for the first opportunity, perhaps at the first break between numbers, and he will ask Bertlef and the young woman to step outside with him for a moment. Once there, he will explain everything, and the unbelievable madness will end.

The musicians finished the first piece, the applause broke out, the nurse said "Excuse me" and left the row, accompanied by Bertlef. Jakub tried to get up to follow them, but Olga grabbed him by the arm and restrained him: "No, please, not now. After intermission!"

It was all so quick he had no time to realize what happened. The musicians had already launched into the next piece, and Jakub understood that the One who was testing him had seated Ruzena nearby not in order to redeem him but in order to confirm his failure and his condemnation beyond all possible doubt.

The trumpeter was blowing, Dr. Skreta was towering over his drums like a great Buddha, and Jakub was sitting immobile in his seat. He saw neither the trumpeter nor Dr. Skreta, he saw only himself, he saw that he was sitting immobile, and he could not tear his eyes away from this horrifying image.

21

When the clear sound of his trumpet resounded in Klima's ears, he believed that it was he himself who was vibrating thus, that he alone was filling the space of the entire hall. He felt strong and invincible.

Ruzena was sitting in the row of complimentary reserved seats, she was sitting next to Bertlef (and that too was a good omen), and the evening's atmosphere was delightful. The audience was listening intently and, above all, in such a good mood that it gave Klima the cautious hope that all would end well. When the applause for the first piece broke out, he pointed with a stylish gesture to Dr. Skreta, who for some reason he found likable and felt close to that evening. The doctor stood up behind his drums and took a bow.

But when he looked into the audience after the second piece, he noticed that Ruzena's seat was empty. This frightened him. From then on he played tensely, running his eyes over the entire hall seat by seat, checking each one but failing to find her. He thought that she had deliberately left in order not to have to hear his arguments once again, having made up her mind not to appear before the Abortion Committee. Where should he look for her after the concert? And what would happen if he failed to find her?

He felt that he was playing badly, mechanically, absentmindedly. But incapable as it was of detecting the trumpeter's gloomy mood, the audience was satisfied and the ovations increased in intensity after each piece.

He reassured himself with the thought that she had merely gone to the toilet. That she was having the sickness common to pregnant women. When half an hour had passed he told himself that she had gone home to get something and would be reappearing in her seat. But after the intermission had gone by and the concert was nearing its end, her seat was still vacant. Perhaps she didn't dare come back into the hall in the middle of the concert. Perhaps she would come back during the final applause.

But now he was hearing the final applause. Ruzena had not appeared, and Klima was at his wits' end. The audience rose and shouted for encores. Klima turned toward Dr. Skreta and shook his head to indicate that he did not want to play anymore. But he was met by a pair of radiant eyes that wanted only to drum, to go on drumming the whole night through.

The audience interpreted Klima's shake of the head as a star's routine flirtatiousness and went on applauding. Just then a beautiful young woman edged her way to the foot of the bandstand, and when he noticed her, Klima thought he was going to collapse, to faint and never reawaken. She smiled at him and said (he could not hear her voice, but he read the words on her lips): "Please play! Please! Please!"

Klima lifted his trumpet to show that he was going to play. The audience instantly quieted.

His two partners were delighted and started to encore the last piece. For Klima it was as if he were playing in the funeral band marching behind his own coffin. He played, and he knew that all was lost, that there was nothing more to do but close his eyes, give up, and let himself be crushed under the wheels of fate.

22

On a small table in Bertlef's suite stood bottles adorned with splendid labels bearing exotic names. Ruzena knew nothing about luxury drinks, and, unable to specify anything else, she asked for whisky.

Her mind, meanwhile, was trying hard to penetrate the veil of giddiness and to understand the situation. She asked Bertlef several times why he had been looking for her today in particular, though he barely knew her. "I want to know," she kept repeating, "I want to know why you thought about me."

"I have been wanting to for a long time," Bertlef answered, gazing steadily into her eyes.

"But why today instead of some other day?"

"Because there is a time for everything. And our time is now."

These words were puzzling, but Ruzena felt they were sincere. The insolubility of her situation had become so intolerable today that something had to happen.

"Yes," she said pensively, "it's been a very strange day."

"You see, you yourself know that I arrived at the right time," Bertlef said in a velvety voice.

Ruzena was overcome by a confused but delightful feeling of relief: Bertlef's appearing precisely today meant that everything that happened had been ordained elsewhere, and she could relax and put herself in the hands of that higher power.

"Yes, it's true, you came at the right time," she said.
"I know it."

And yet there was still something that escaped her: "But why? Why were you looking for me?"

"Because I love you."

The word "love" was uttered very softly, but the room was suddenly filled with it.

Ruzena lowered her voice: "You love me?"

"Yes, I love you."

Frantisek and Klima had already said the word to her, but only now did she see it as it really is when it comes unasked for, unexpected, naked. The word entered the room like a miracle. It was totally inexplicable, but to Ruzena it seemed all the more real, for the most basic things in this world exist without explanation and without motive, drawing from within themselves their reason for being.

"Really?" she asked, and her voice, usually too loud, was only a whisper.

"Yes, really."

"But I'm a very ordinary girl."

"Not at all"

"Yes, I am."

"You are beautiful."

"No, I'm not."

"You are tender."

"No," she said, shaking her head.

"You radiate kindness and goodness."

She shook her head: "No, no, no."

"I know what you are. I know it better than you do."

"You don't know anything about it."

"Yes, I do."

The confidence in her that was emanating from Bertlef's eyes was like a magical bath, and Ruzena wished that gaze, which flooded over and caressed her, to go on for as long as possible.

"Is it true? That I'm like that?"

"Yes. I know you are."

It was as beautiful as a vertigo: in Bertlef's eyes she felt herself delicate, tender, pure, she felt as noble as a queen. It was like being suddenly gorged with honey and fragrant herbs. She found herself adorable. (My God, she had never before found herself so delightfully adorable!)

She continued to protest: "But you hardly know me."

"I have known you for a long time. I have been watching you for a long time, and you never even suspected it. I know you by heart," he said, running his fingers over her face. "Your nose, your delicately drawn smile, your hair . . ."

Then he started to unbutton her clothes, and she did not resist at all, she merely looked deeply into his eyes, into that gaze that enveloped her like water, like velvety water. She was sitting facing him, her bare breasts rising under his gaze and desiring to be seen and praised. Her whole body was turned toward his eyes like a sunflower toward the sun.

23

They were in Jakub's room, Olga talking and Jakub repeating to himself that there was still time. He could return to Karl Marx House, and if she was not there he could disturb Bertlef in the suite next door and ask him if he knew where the young woman had gone.

Olga chattered on, and he went on to imagine the painful scene in which, having found the nurse, he was telling her something or other, stammering, making excuses, apologizing, and trying to get her to give him the tube of tablets. Then, all of a sudden, as if wearied by these visions that for several hours had been confronting him, he felt gripped by an intense indifference.

This was not merely the indifference of weariness, it was a deliberate and combative indifference. Jakub came to realize that it was absolutely all the same to him whether the creature with the yellow hair lived or died, and that it would in fact be hypocrisy and shameful playacting if he tried to save her. That he would actually be deceiving the One who was testing him. For the One who was testing him (God, who did not exist) wished to know Jakub as he really was, not as he pretended to be. And Jakub resolved to be honest with Him; to be who he really was.

They were sitting in facing armchairs, with a small table between them. Jakub saw Olga leaning toward him over that small table and heard her voice: "I want to kiss you. How can we have known each other such a long time and never kissed?"

24

With a forced smile on her face and anxiety deep down within her, Mrs. Klima slipped into the artists' room behind her husband. She was afraid of seeing the actual face of Klima's mistress. But there was no mistress at all. There were several girls flittering around Klima asking for autographs, and she discerned (she had an eagle eye) that none of them knew him personally.

All the same she was certain that the mistress was somewhere nearby. She could see it on Klima's face, which was pale and absent. He smiled at his wife as falsely as she smiled at him.

Dr. Skreta, the pharmacist, and some others, probably physicians and their spouses, introduced themselves to Mrs. Klima with nods. Someone suggested they go to the only bar in town. Klima excused himself, claiming fatigue. Mrs. Klima thought that the mistress must be waiting in the bar; that was why Klima was refusing to go there. And because calamity attracted her like a magnet, she asked him to please her by overcoming his fatigue.

But in the bar, too, there was no woman she might suspect of having an affair with Klima. They sat down at a large table. Dr. Skreta was garrulously praising the trumpeter. The pharmacist was filled with shy happiness he was unable to express. Mrs. Klima tried to be charming and cheerfully talkative: "Doctor, you were magnificent," she said to Skreta, "and you, too, my dear pharmacist. And the atmosphere was genuine, cheerful, carefree, a thousand times better than at the concerts in the capital."

Without staring at Klima, she did not for a second stop observing him. She felt that he was hiding his nervousness only with great effort, and that he was uttering a word now and again only to avoid showing that his mind was elsewhere. It was obvious that she had spoiled something for him, something out of the ordinary. If it had been only a matter of some ordinary adventure (Klima always swore up and down to her that he could never fall in love with another woman), he would not have gone into such a deep depression. Admittedly she had not seen the mistress, but she believed she was seeing the love; the love in his face (suffering, desperate love), and that sight was perhaps still more painful.

"What's the matter, Mister Klima?" suddenly asked the pharmacist, who was all the more friendly and perceptive for being so quiet.

"Nothing. Nothing at all!" said Klima, struck by fear. "I've got a little headache."

"Do you want an aspirin?" the pharmacist asked.

"No, no," said the trumpeter, shaking his head. "But please excuse us if we leave a bit early. I'm really very tired."

25

How had she finally dared to do it?

From the moment she had joined Jakub in the brasserie, she found him not as he had been. He was quiet yet pleasant, unable to focus attention yet docile, was mentally elsewhere yet did whatever she wished. The lack of concentration (she attributed it to his approaching departure) was agreeable to her: she was speaking to an absent face, and it seemed to her that she was speaking into distances where she could not be heard. She could thus say to him what she had never said before.

Now, in asking him for a kiss, she had the impression that she had disturbed him, troubled him. But this did not discourage her at all, on the contrary, it pleased her: she felt she had finally become the bold, provocative woman she had always hoped to be, the woman who dominates the situation, sets it in motion, watches her partner with curiosity, and puts him into a quandary.

She continued to look him firmly in the eye and said

with a smile: "But not here. It would be ridiculous for us to lean over the table to kiss. Come."

She took his hand, led him to the daybed, and savored the finesse, elegance, and quiet authority of her behavior. Then she kissed him and was stirred by a passion she had never known before. And yet it was not the spontaneous passion of a body unable to control itself, it was a passion of the brain, a passion conscious and deliberate. She wanted to tear away from Jakub the disguise of his paternal role, wanted to shock him and arouse herself with the sight of his confusion, wanted to rape him and watch herself raping him, wanted to know the taste of his tongue and feel his paternal hands become bit by bit bolder and cover her with caresses.

She unbuttoned his jacket and took it off.

26

He never took his eyes off him throughout the concert, and then he mingled with the fans who rushed behind the bandstand to get the artists to scribble an autograph for them. But Ruzena was not there. He followed a small group of people leading the trumpeter to the spa town's bar. He went in behind them, convinced that Ruzena was already waiting there for the trumpeter. But he was wrong. He went out and for a long time kept watch in front of the entrance.

A sudden pang went through him. The trumpeter had come out of the bar with a female figure pressed against him. At first he thought it was Ruzena, but it was not she.

He followed them to the Hotel Richmond, and Klima and the woman vanished inside.

He quickly went across the park to Karl Marx House. The door was still unlocked. He asked the doorkeeper if Ruzena was at home. She was not.

He ran back to the Richmond, fearing that Ruzena in the meantime had joined Klima there. He paced back and forth on the park path, keeping his eyes fixed on the entrance. He didn't understand what was happening. Several possibilities came to his mind, but they didn't matter. What mattered was that he was here and that he was keeping watch, and he knew that he would keep watch until he saw them.

Why? What good would it do? Would it not be better to go home to sleep?

He repeated to himself that he finally had to find out the whole truth.

But did he really want to know the truth? Did he really wish so strongly to make sure that Ruzena was going to bed with Klima? Was he not waiting instead for some proof of Ruzena's innocence? And yet, suspicious as he was, would he lend credence to such proof?

He didn't know what he was waiting for. He knew only that he would wait a long time, all night if he had to, and even several nights. For time spurred on by jealousy passes with amazing speed. Jealousy occupies the mind more completely than passionate intellectual work. The mind has not a moment of leisure. A victim of jealousy never knows boredom.

Frantisek keeps pacing a short stretch of path, barely one hundred meters long, from which the Richmond's entrance can be seen. He is going to be pacing back and forth like this all night, until everyone else is asleep, he is going to pace back and forth like this until tomorrow, until the last part of this book.

But why is he not sitting down? There are benches facing the Richmond!

He cannot sit down. Jealousy is like a raging toothache. One cannot do anything when one is jealous, not even sit down. One can only come and go. Back and forth.

27

They followed the same route as Bertlef and Ruzena, Jakub and Olga; up the stairs to the second floor, then along the red plush carpet to the corridor's end at the large door to Bertlef's suite. To the right was the door to Jakub's room, to the left the room Dr. Skreta had lent to Klima.

When he opened the door and turned on the light, he noticed the quick inquisitive look Kamila cast through the room. He knew she was looking for traces of a woman. He was familiar with that look. He knew everything about her. He knew that her kindness was insincere. He knew that she had come here to spy on him, knew that she would pretend to have come here to please him. And he knew that she clearly perceived his embarrassment and that she was certain she had spoiled one of his love adventures.

"Darling, you really don't mind that I came?" she asked.

"Why should I mind?"

"I was afraid you'd be sad here."

"Yes, without you I'd be sad. It pleased me to see you applauding at the foot of the bandstand."

"You seem tired. Or is something bothering you?"

"No. No, nothing's bothering me. I'm just tired."

"You're sad because you're always surrounded by men here. But now you're with a beautiful woman. Am I not a beautiful woman?"

"Yes, you're a beautiful woman," answered Klima, and these were the first sincere words he had said to her that day. Kamila was gloriously beautiful, and Klima felt immense pain at the thought that this beauty was exposed to mortal peril. But this beauty smiled at him and began to undress before his eyes. He gazed at her body being bared, and it was as if he were bidding it farewell. The breasts, her beautiful, flawless breasts, her narrow waist, the belly from which her underpants had just slipped free. He watched her with longing, as if she were a memory. As if through a window. As if from a distance. Her nakedness was so distant that he felt not the least aroused. And yet he was contemplating her with a voracious gaze. He drank her nakedness as a condemned man drinks his last glass. He drank her nakedness as a man drinks a lost past, a lost life.

Kamila came near him: "What is it? Aren't you going to undress?"

All he could do was undress, and he was terribly sad.

"Don't think you have the right to be tired now that I've come all this way to be with you. I want you."

He knew that it was not true. He knew that Kamila did not have the slightest desire to make love, and that she was forcing herself to behave provocatively only because she saw his sadness and attributed it to his love for another woman. He knew (my God, how well he knew her!) that she was trying to test him with this love challenge, to find out to what degree his mind was engrossed by another woman, he knew that she wanted to wound herself with his sadness.

"I'm really tired," he said.

She took him in her arms and then led him to the bed: "You'll see how I'm going to make you forget your fatigue!" And she began to play with his naked body.

He was stretched out as if on an operating table. He knew that all his wife's efforts would be useless. His body shrank into itself and no longer had the slightest power of expansion. Kamila ran her moist lips all over his body, and he knew that she wanted to make herself suffer and make him suffer, and he hated her. He hated her with all the intensity of his love: it was she and she alone, with her jealousy, her suspicions, her mistrust, she and she alone who had spoiled everything by coming here today, it was because of her that their marriage was menaced by a bomb deposited in another woman's belly, by a charge timed to blow everything up in seven months. It was she and she alone, with her insane fear about their love, who had destroyed everything.

She put her mouth to his belly and felt his member contract under her touches, going back inside, fleeing from her, becoming more and more small and anxious. And he knew that Kamila saw the rejection of her body as a measure of the extent of his love for another woman. He knew that she was suffering, and that the more she suffered the more she would make him suffer and persist in putting her moist lips to his powerless body.

28

He had never wanted to go to bed with this girl. He desired to make her happy and shower her with goodness, but this goodness had nothing in common with sensual desire, better still, it totally excluded such desire, for it wished to be pure, disinterested, detached from all pleasure.

But what could he do now? Must he, in order not to sully his goodness, reject Olga? He knew he could not do that. His rejection would hurt Olga and would mark her for a long time. He realized that he must drink the chalice of goodness to the dregs.

And then she was suddenly naked in front of him and he told himself that her face was noble and pleasing. But that was small comfort when he saw the face together with the body, which looked like a long thin stem topped by an inordinately big, long-haired flower.

But whether she was beautiful or not, Jakub knew that there was no escape. Besides, he felt that his body (that servile body) was once more quite willing to lift its obliging spear. His arousal, however, seemed to him to be happening to someone else far away, outside his own soul, as if he were being aroused without his participation and were secretly scorning it. His soul was far from his body, obsessed by the thought of the poison in the woman's handbag. At the utmost, it watched regretfully as the body blindly and pitilessly pursued its trivial interests.

A fleeting memory passed through his mind: he had been ten years old when he learned how children come into the world, and since then the thought of it had increasingly haunted him, all the more when, over the years, he gradually discovered the actual substance of the female organs. Since then he had often imagined his own birth; he imagined his tiny body sliding through a narrow, wet tunnel, he imagined his nose and his mouth full of the strange mucus he was entirely anointed with and marked by. Yes, that female mucus had marked Jakub throughout his life with its ability to exert its mysterious power to summon him to it at any moment and to control the bizarre mechanisms of his body. This had always been repugnant to him, and he rebelled against that servitude by at least refusing to give women his soul, by safeguarding his freedom and solitude, by restricting mucus power to particular hours of his life. Yes, his great affection for Olga probably derived from her being sexually out of bounds to him, and from his certainty that her body would never remind him of the shameful way he had come into the world.

He abruptly pushed these thoughts away, because the situation on the daybed was developing rapidly, and in a moment or two he was going to have to enter her body, and he did not wish to do so with a sensation of repugnance. He told himself that this woman opening herself up to him was the only woman to whom he was attached by pure and disinterested affection, and that he was now going to make love to her only to make her happy, to please her, to make her self-confident and cheerful.

But now he amazed himself: he was moving on top of her as if he were rocking on waves of goodness. He felt happy, he felt good. His soul humbly identified itself with the activity of his body, as if the act of love were merely the physical expression of a kindly tenderness, of a pure feeling toward one's neighbor. There was no obstacle, not a false note. They held each other tightly, and their breaths mingled.

Those were long, beautiful minutes, and then Olga whispered a lewd word in his ear. She whispered it once, then again and yet again, arousing herself with the word.

The waves of goodness suddenly ebbed, and Jakub and the young woman found themselves in the middle of a desert.

No, Jakub ordinarily had nothing against lewd words during lovemaking. They awakened his sensuality and ferocity. They made women pleasantly strange to his soul, pleasantly desirable to his body.

But the lewd word coming from Olga's mouth brutally destroyed the whole sweet illusion. It woke him from a dream. The haze of goodness lifted, and suddenly he saw Olga in his arms as he had seen her a while earlier: with the big flower of her head atop the swaying thin stem of her body. This touching creature had the provocative manner of a whore without ceasing to be touching, so that the lewd words sounded ridiculous and sad.

But Jakub knew that he must not let anything show, that he must control himself, that he must drink the bitter chalice of goodness again and again, because this absurd embrace was his only good deed, his only redemption (not for a moment did he forget the poison in that woman's handbag), his only salvation.

29

Like a large pearl in a mollusk's double shell, Bertlef's luxurious suite is surrounded on both sides by the less luxurious rooms occupied by Jakub and Klima. In these two neighboring rooms silence and calm have been reigning for quite a while, as Ruzena, in Bertlef's arms, heaves her last sighs of voluptuous pleasure.

Then she lies stretched out peacefully beside him as he caresses her face. She soon bursts into tears. She cries for a long time, her head buried in his chest.

Bertlef caresses her as if she were a little girl, and she really does feel little. Little as never before (never before has she hidden this way in anyone's chest), but also big as never before (never before has she experienced so much pleasure). And the spasmodic movements of her sobs carry her away to sensations of well-being which until now had been equally unknown to her.

Where is Klima at this moment, and where is Frantisek? They are somewhere in a distant haze, figures as light as feathers receding toward the horizon. And where is Ruzena's stubborn longing to grab hold of one and get rid of the other? What has become of her fits of anger, of the offended silence she has locked herself into since morning?

She is lying down, she is sobbing, and he is caressing her face. He tells her to sleep, that his bed is in the next room. Ruzena opens her eyes and looks at him: naked,

Bertlef goes to the bathroom (the sound of running water is heard), then he returns, opens the wardrobe, takes out a blanket, and delicately unfolds it over Ruzena's body.

Ruzena sees the varicose veins on his calves. When he is bent over her she notices that his curly hair is graying and thin enough to let the scalp show through. Bertlef is sixty, perhaps sixty-five, but that is not important to Ruzena. On the contrary, his age calms her, his age throws a radiant light on her own still dull and expressionless youth, and she feels full of life and that she has finally arrived at the very beginning of her journey. And here in his presence is where she finds out that she will still be young for a long time, that she has no need to hurry. Bertlef again sits down beside her and caresses her, and she has the sense of having found refuge not only in the comforting touch of his fingers but also in the reassuring embrace of his years.

Then she loses consciousness, the confused visions of sleep's approach passing through her head. She awakes, and it seems to her that the whole room is flooded with a strange blue light. What is this unnatural glow she has never before seen? Has the moon come down here veiled in blue? Or is Ruzena dreaming with her eyes open?

Bertlef smiles at her and goes on caressing her face.

And now she closes her eyes for the night, carried away by a dream.

Fifth Day

1

It was still dark when Klima awoke from a very light sleep. He wanted to find Ruzena before she went to work. But how to explain to Kamila that he had an errand to run before daybreak?

He looked at his watch: five o'clock. He would miss Ruzena if he did not get up right away, but he could not think of an excuse. His heart pounded, but unable to do anything else, he got up and started to dress, quietly for fear of waking Kamila. He was buttoning his jacket when he heard her voice. It was a high-pitched, half-asleep little voice: "Where are you going?"

He went over to the bed and lightly kissed her lips: "Go back to sleep, I'll be back soon."

"I'll go with you," said Kamila, but she was instantly asleep again.

Klima quickly left.

2

Was it possible? Was he still pacing back and forth?

Yes. But suddenly he stopped. He saw Klima coming out of the Richmond. He hid briefly and then started to follow him discreetly to Karl Marx House. He passed the doorkeeper's lodging (the doorkeeper was asleep) and stopped at the corner of the corridor leading to Ruzena's room. He saw the trumpeter knock at the nurse's door. The door did not open. Klima knocked several more times, then he turned to go.

Frantisek rushed out of Marx House after him. He saw him heading down the park to the thermal building, where Ruzena was due to begin work in half an hour. He rushed back to Marx House, hammered at Ruzena's door, and in a hushed but distinct voice said through the keyhole: "It's me! Frantisek! Don't be afraid of me! You can open the door for me!"

There was no answer.

As he left, the doorkeeper was waking up.

"Is Ruzena at home?" Frantisek asked him.

"She hasn't been here since yesterday," said the doorkeeper.

Frantisek went outside. In the distance he saw Klima entering the thermal building.

3

Ruzena regularly awoke at five-thirty. Even this morning, after having dozed off so pleasantly, she slept no longer than that. She got up, dressed, and tiptoed into the adjacent room.

Bertlef was lying on his side, breathing deeply, and his hair, always carefully combed during the day, was disheveled, revealing the naked skin over his skull. In sleep his face looked grayer and older. The small bottles of medicine on the night table reminded Ruzena of a hospital. But none of this disturbed her. Looking at him brought tears to her eyes. She had never had a more beautiful night. She felt a strange desire to kneel down before him. She did not do so, but she leaned over and delicately kissed his brow.

Outside, as she approached the thermal building she saw Frantisek coming toward her.

The day before, such an encounter would have disconcerted her. Even though Ruzena was in love with the trumpeter, Frantisek meant a great deal to her. He and Klima formed an inseparable pair. One embodied the everyday, the other a dream; one wanted her, the other did not want her; from one she wanted to escape, the other she desired. Each of the two men determined the meaning of the other's existence. When she decided that she was pregnant by Klima she did not eliminate Frantisek from her life; on the contrary: Frantisek remained the abiding reason for this decision. She was between these two men as between the two poles of her life; they were the north and south of her planet, the only one she knew.

But this morning she suddenly realized that it was not the only habitable planet. She realized that it was possible to live without Klima and without Frantisek; that there was no reason to hurry; that there was time enough; that it was possible to let a wise, mature man lead you far away from this accursed domain where you age so quickly.

"Where did you spend the night?" Frantisek burst out at her.

"It's none of your business."

"I was at your place. You weren't in your room."

"It's absolutely none of your business where I spent the night," said Ruzena, and without stopping she passed through the entrance to the thermal building. "And quit following me. I forbid it."

Frantisek remained standing in front of the building, and then, because his feet hurt from a night spent pacing back and forth, he sat down on a bench from which he could keep a close watch on the entrance.

Ruzena rushed up the stairs to the second floor two at a time and entered the large waiting room lined with benches and chairs. Klima was sitting at the door to her workplace.

"Ruzena," he said as he stood up and looked at her with desperate eyes. "I beg you. I beg you, be reasonable! I'll go there with you!"

His anxiety was naked, stripped of all the sentimental demagogy to which he had devoted so much effort in the previous days.

Ruzena said: "You want to get rid of me."

This frightened him: "I don't want to get rid of you—on the contrary. I'm doing all this so we'll be even happier together."

"Don't lie," said Ruzena.

"Ruzena, I beg you! It'll be a disaster if you don't go!"

"Who told you I'm not going? We still have three hours. It's only six o'clock. You can quietly get back into bed with your wife!"

She closed the door behind her, put on her white smock, and said to the fortyish nurse: "Please do me a favor. I need to go out at nine o'clock. Could you take my place for an hour?"

"So you've let yourself be talked into it after all," her colleague said reproachfully.

"No. I've fallen in love," said Ruzena.

4

Jakub went over to the window and opened it. He thought of the pale-blue tablet, and he could not believe that he had really given it the day before to a stranger. He looked up at the blue of the sky and breathed in the crisp air of the autumn morning. The

world he saw through the window was normal, tran-
quil, natural. The episode with the nurse the day
before suddenly seemed absurd and implausible.

He picked up the phone and dialed the thermal
building. He asked to speak with Nurse Ruzena in the
women's section. He waited a long time. Then he heard
a woman's voice. He repeated that he wanted to speak
with Nurse Ruzena. The voice replied that Nurse
Ruzena was now at the pool and couldn't come to the
phone. He thanked her and hung up.

He felt immense relief: the nurse was alive. The
tablets in the tube were to be taken three times a day;
she must have taken one yesterday evening and
another this morning, and thus she had swallowed
Jakub's tablet quite a while ago. Suddenly everything
seemed absolutely clear: the pale-blue tablet he had
been carrying in his pocket as a guarantee of his freedom was a fraud. His friend had given him a tablet of
illusion.

My God, why had the thought not occurred to him
before? Once more he recalled the distant day when he
had asked his friends for poison. He had just been
released from prison then, and now he realized, after
the passage of many long years, that all of them had
probably seen his request as a theatrical gesture
designed to call attention, after the fact, to the sufferings he had endured. But Skreta had with no hesitation
promised to get him what he asked for, and a few days
later had brought him a shiny, pale-blue tablet. Why
hesitate, why try to dissuade him? Skreta had handled

it more cleverly than those who had turned him down. He had furnished him the harmless illusion of calm and certainty, and in addition made a lifelong friend.

Why had this thought never occurred to him? He had at the time found it a bit strange that Skreta had furnished him the poison in the guise of an ordinary manufactured tablet. While he knew that Skreta, as a biochemist, had access to poisons, he did not understand how he had tablet-making machinery at his disposal. But he asked no questions. Although he doubted everything else, he believed in his tablet as one believes in the Gospel.

Now, in this moment of immense relief, he was of course grateful to his friend for his fraud. He was happy that the nurse was alive and that the whole absurd misadventure was merely a nightmare, a bad dream. But nothing lasts long in this world, and behind the subsiding waves of relief, regret raised its shrill voice:

How grotesque! The tablet he kept in his pocket had given his every step a theatrical solemnity and allowed him to turn his life into a grandiose myth! He had been convinced that he was carrying death with him in a piece of tissue paper that in reality held only Skreta's stifled laughter.

Jakub knew that, when all is said and done, his friend had been right, but he could not help thinking that the Skreta he loved so much had suddenly become an ordinary doctor like thousands of others. His having furnished him the poison with no hesitation, as a matter of course, radically distinguished him from other people Jakub knew. There was something implausible about his behavior. He did not act the way other people did. He had not even wondered if Jakub might misuse the poison in a fit of hysteria or depression. He had dealt with Jakub as a man who was in total control of himself and had no human weaknesses. They behaved with each other like two gods forced to live among humans—and that was beautiful. Unforgettable. And suddenly it was over.

Jakub looked up at the blue of the sky and thought: Today he brought me relief and calm. And at the same time he robbed me of himself; he robbed me of my Skreta.

5

Ruzena's consent put Klima into a sweet stupor, but nothing could have lured him away from the waiting room. Ruzena's baffling disappearance the day before was threateningly imprinted on his memory. He resolved to wait there patiently, to see to it that no one dissuaded her or carried her away.

Women patients began to arrive, opening the door behind which Ruzena had vanished just now, some of them staying in there and others returning to sit in the chairs along the walls and examine Klima curiously, for men were not usually seen in the women's section waiting room.

Next a buxom woman in a white smock came in and took a long look at him; then she approached him and asked if he was waiting for Ruzena. He blushed and nodded.

"You don't have to wait here. You've got till nine o'clock," she said with obtrusive familiarity, and Klima had the impression that all the women in the room heard her and knew what was going on.

It was a quarter to nine when Ruzena reappeared, dressed in street clothes. He went behind her as they silently left the thermal building. They were both immersed in their own thoughts and did not notice that Frantisek was following them, hidden by the park's bushes.

6

Jakub had nothing more to do but say goodbye to Olga and Skreta, but first he wanted to take (for the last time) a brief walk by himself in the park and have a nostalgic look at the flaming trees.

Just as he was coming out into the corridor a young woman was locking the door of the room opposite, and her tall figure caught his eye. When she turned around he was stunned by her beauty.

He spoke to her: "Aren't you a friend of Doctor Skreta's?"

The woman smiled pleasantly: "How did you know?"

"You've just left the room he reserves for his friends," said Jakub and introduced himself.

"I'm glad to meet you. I'm Mrs. Klima. The doctor put up my husband here. I'm going to look for him. He must be with the doctor. Do you know where I might find them?"

Jakub contemplated the young woman with insatiable delight, and it occurred to him (yet again!) that this was his last day here, which imparted special significance to every event and turned it into a symbolic message.

But what did the message say?

"I can take you to Doctor Skreta," Jakub told her.

"I'd be very grateful," she replied.

Yes, what did the message say?

First of all, it was only a message and nothing more. In two hours Jakub would be going away, and nothing would be left for him of this beautiful creature. This woman had appeared before him as a denial. He had met her only to be convinced that she could not be his. He had met her as an image of everything he would lose by his departure.

"It's extraordinary," he said. "Today I'm probably going to be talking to Doctor Skreta for the last time in my life."

But the message this woman had brought him also said something more. The message had arrived, at the very last moment, to announce beauty to him. Yes, beauty, and Jakub was startled to realize that he actually knew nothing about beauty, that he had spent his life ignoring it and never living for it. The beauty of this woman fascinated him. He suddenly had the feeling that in all his decisions there had always been an error. That there was an element he had forgotten to take into account. It seemed to him that if he had known this woman, his decision would have been different.

"Why are you going to be talking to him for the last time?"

"I'm going abroad. For a long time."

Not that he had not had pretty women, but their charm was always something incidental for him. What drove him toward women was a desire for revenge, or sadness and dissatisfaction, or compassion, or pity: the world of women merged for him with his country's bitter drama, in which he had participated both as persecutor and victim, and had experienced plenty of struggle and no idylls. But this woman had sprung up before him suddenly, separate from all that, separate from his life, she had come from outside, she had appeared to him, appeared not only as a beautiful woman but as beauty itself, and she proclaimed to him that one could live here in a different way and for something different, that beauty is more than justice, that beauty is more than truth, that it is more real, more indisputable, and also more accessible, that beauty is superior to everything else and that it was now permanently lost to him. This beautiful woman had shown herself to him so that he would not go on believing that he knew everything and had exhausted all the possibilities of life here.

"I envy you," she said.

They crossed the park together, the sky was blue, the bushes were yellow and red, and Jakub again thought that the foliage was the image of a fire consuming all the adventures, all the memories, all the opportunities of his past.

"There's nothing to envy me for. Right now I feel I shouldn't be leaving at all."

"Why not? Are you starting to like it here at the last minute?"

"It's you I like. I like you a lot. You're extremely beautiful."

He was surprised to hear himself say this, and then it came to him that he had the right to tell her everything because he would be leaving in a few hours and his words could have no consequences either for him or for her. This suddenly discovered freedom intoxicated him.

"I've been living like a blind man. A blind man. Now, for the first time, I realize that beauty exists. And that I went right by it."

She merged in his mind with music and paintings, with a realm in which he had never set foot, she merged with the multicolored foliage around him, and all of a sudden he no longer saw in it any messages or significance (images of fire or incineration) but only the ecstasy of beauty mysteriously awakened by the beat of her footsteps, by the touch of her voice.

"I'd do anything to win you. I'd abandon everything and live my whole life differently, only for you and because of you. But I can't, because at this moment I'm no longer really here. I should have left yesterday, and I'm only here now through my own delay."

Ah yes! Now he understood why it had been given him to meet her. This meeting was taking place outside his life, somewhere on the hidden side of his destiny, on the reverse of his biography. But he spoke to her all the more freely, until he suddenly felt that, even so, he would be unable to say everything he wanted to say.

He touched her arm: "This is where Doctor Skreta has his office. On the second floor."

Mrs. Klima gave him a long look, and Jakub plunged into that look, tender and misty like a distance. He touched her arm again, turned, and went off.

A bit later he turned around and saw that Mrs. Klima was still standing in the same spot, following him with her eyes. He turned around several more times; she was still looking at him.

7

About twenty anxious women were sitting in the waiting room; Ruzena and Klima could find no seats. On the wall facing them hung the obligatory big posters aiming to dissuade women from having abortions.

MAMA, WHY DON'T YOU WANT ME? read the large letters on a poster showing a smiling baby in a crib; below the baby, in heavy letters, was a poem in which an embryo implores its mama not to scrape it away and promises boundless joy in return: "*. . . If you don't let me stay alive—oh why?/Whose arms, Mama, will hold you when you die?*"

Other posters displayed big photos of smiling mothers pushing baby carriages and photos of little boys peeing. (Klima thought that a little boy peeing was an irrefutable argument for childbearing. He remembered once seeing a film in which a little boy was peeing, and the whole theater quivered with blissful female sighs.)

After waiting a while, Klima knocked on the door; a nurse came out and Klima dropped Dr. Skreta's name. In a moment the doctor arrived and handed Klima a form, asking him to fill it out and wait patiently a while longer.

Klima held the form against the wall and started to fill it out: name, date of birth, place of birth. Ruzena whispered her responses. Then he came to FATHER'S NAME, and he hesitated. It was horrifying to see this infamous title in black and white, and to put his name next to it.

Ruzena noticed that Klima's hand was trembling. That gave her great satisfaction: "Go on, write!" she said.

"What name should I put down?" Klima whispered.

She found him spineless and cowardly, and she was filled with contempt for him. He was afraid of everything, afraid of responsibility, afraid of his own signature on an official form.

"Come on! I think you know who the father is!" she said.

"I thought it wasn't important," said Klima.

She no longer cared about him, but deep down she was convinced that this spineless fellow was guilty of doing her harm; it delighted her to punish him: "If you're going to keep on lying, we're not going to get along." After he had written his name in the space, she added with a sigh: "Anyway, I still don't know what I'm going to do . . ."

"What?"

She looked at his terrified face: "Until they take it away from me, I can still change my mind."

8

She was sitting in an armchair with her legs extended on the table, and she was skimming the detective novel she had bought for all the dreary days in the spa town. But she could not concentrate because the situations and words of the evening before kept coming to mind. Everything had pleased her yesterday, particularly she herself. At last she was what she had always wished to be: no longer the victim of male intentions but the author of her own adventure. She had definitively rejected the role of innocent ward which Jakub had made her play, and, on the contrary, she had remodeled him in accord with her own wishes.

She now felt elegant, independent, and bold. She looked at her legs up on the table, sheathed in tight white jeans, and when she heard a knock on the door she shouted cheerfully: "Come in, I'm waiting for you!"

Jakub entered, looking distressed.

"Hello!" she said, keeping her legs on the table for a moment. Jakub seemed perplexed, and that pleased her. She got up, went over to him, and lightly kissed him on the cheek: "Will you stay a while?"

"No," said Jakub sadly. "This time I've come to say goodbye for good. I'm leaving very soon. I thought I'd take you to the baths one last time."

"Sure!" said Olga cheerfully. "Let's go for a walk."

9

Jakub was filled to overflowing with the image of the beautiful Mrs. Klima, and he needed to overcome a kind of aversion to come and say goodbye to Olga, who the day before had left his soul uneasy and blemished. But not for anything would he let her see this. He enjoined himself to behave with extraordinary tact, that she must not suspect how little pleasure and joy their lovemaking had brought him, that her memory of him should remain unspoiled. He put on a serious air, uttered insignificant phrases in a melancholy tone, vaguely touched her hand and caressed her hair, and, when she looked into his eyes, tried to appear sad.

On the way she suggested that they stop for a glass of wine, but Jakub wanted to keep their last meeting, which he found difficult, as brief as possible. "Saying farewell hurts too much. I don't want to prolong it," he said.

In front of the thermal building he took both of her hands and looked into her eyes for a long while.

Olga said: "Jakub, it was very good of you to have come here. I spent a delightful evening yesterday. I'm glad that you've finally stopped playing papa and become Jakub. Yesterday was fantastic. Wasn't it fantastic?"

Jakub understood that he understood nothing. Did this sensitive girl see last evening's lovemaking simply as entertainment? Was she driven toward him by a sensuality free from all feelings? Did the pleasant memory of a single night of love outweigh for her the sadness of final separation?

He gave her a kiss. She wished him a pleasant journey and vanished through the building's grand entrance.

10

He had been pacing back and forth in front of the clinic building for two hours, and he was starting to lose patience. He kept reminding himself that he must not make a scene, but he felt that his self-control was waning.

He went inside. The spa was a small place, and everyone knew him. He asked the doorkeeper if he had seen Ruzena. The doorkeeper nodded and said that she had gone up in the elevator. Since the elevator only stopped at the fourth floor and all the lower floors were reached by stairs, Frantisek could narrow his suspicions to the two corridors on the top floor. In one were offices, in the other was the gynecology clinic. He tried the former first (it was deserted) and then entered the latter, with the unpleasant feeling that men were not allowed here. He saw a nurse he knew by sight. He asked her about Ruzena. She pointed to a door at the end of the corridor. The door was open, and some women and men stood waiting at the threshold. Frantisek went in and saw more women sitting, but neither Ruzena nor the trumpeter was there.

"Did anybody see a young woman, a blonde?"

A woman pointed to the office door: "They're inside."

Frantisek looked up: MAMA, WHY DON'T YOU WANT ME? And on the other posters he saw the photographs of newborns and little boys urinating. He began to understand what was going on.

11

There was a long table in the room. Klima sat beside Ruzena, and facing them Dr. Skreta sat enthroned, flanked by two ample ladies.

Dr. Skreta lifted his eyes to the applicants and shook his head with disgust: "It makes me sick even to look at you. Do you know how much trouble we go to here to restore fertility to unfortunate women who can't have children? And then healthy, well-built young people like you of their own accord want to get rid of the most precious gift life can offer us. I warn you categorically that this committee is not here to encourage abortions but to regulate them."

The two women emitted grunts of approval, and Dr. Skreta went on giving his moral lesson for the benefit of the two applicants. Klima's heart was pounding. He guessed that the doctor's words were not addressed to him but to the two judges, who with all the strength of their maternal bellies hated young women who refused to give birth, yet he feared that Ruzena might allow herself to be swayed by this speech. Had she not told him a few minutes earlier that she still didn't know what she was going to do?

"What are you living for?" Dr. Skreta resumed. "Life without children is like a tree without leaves. If I had the power I would prohibit abortion. Aren't you distressed by the thought that our population is going down each year? Here in this country where mothers and children are better protected than anywhere else in the world! In this country where no one has to fear for his future?"

The two women once again emitted grunts of approval, and Dr. Skreta went on: "The comrade is married and afraid of assuming all the consequences of an irresponsible sexual relationship. But you should have thought of that before, comrade!"

Dr. Skreta paused, and then he addressed Klima once more: "You have no children. Are you really unable to get a divorce for the sake of this fetus's future?"

"It's impossible," said Klima.

"I know," said Dr. Skreta with a sigh. "I've received a psychiatric report saying that Mrs. Klima suffers from suicidal tendencies. The birth of this child would endanger her life and destroy her home, and Nurse Ruzena would be a single mother. What can we do?" he said with another sigh, and then pushed the form toward one and then the other of the two women, each one sighing too as she signed her name in the proper space.

"Be here Monday morning at eight o'clock for the operation," Dr. Skreta said to Ruzena, and he motioned that she could leave.

"But you stay here!" one of the heavy women said to Klima. Ruzena left and the woman went on: "Terminating a pregnancy is not as harmless an operation as you think. It involves much bleeding. By your irresponsibility you will make the comrade lose blood, and it's only fair that you give your own." She pushed a form at Klima and told him: "Sign here."

Filled with confusion, Klima signed obediently.

"It's an application for membership in the Voluntary Association of Blood Donors. Go next door and the nurse will take your blood right away."

12

Ruzena walked through the waiting room with lowered eyes and didn't see Frantisek until he spoke to her in the corridor.

"Where have you just been?"

She was frightened by his furious expression and walked faster.

"I'm asking you where you've just been."

"It's none of your business."

"I know where you've just been."

"Then don't ask me."

They went down the stairs, Ruzena in a rush to escape Frantisek and the conversation.

"You've been to the Abortion Committee," Frantisek said.

Ruzena remained silent. They left the building.

"You've been to the Abortion Committee. I know it. And you want to have an abortion."

"I'll do what I want."

"You're not going to do what you want. It's my business too."

Ruzena was walking still faster, nearly running.
Frantisek was running right behind her. When they
arrived at the thermal building, she said: "I forbid you
to follow me. I'm at work now. You don't have the right
to disturb me at my work."

Frantisek was very excited: "I forbid you to give me
orders!"

"You don't have the right!"

"You're the one who doesn't have the right!"

Ruzena swept into the building, with Frantisek
behind her.

13

Jakub was glad that it was all finished and that there
was only one more thing to do: say goodbye to Skreta.
From the thermal building he slowly headed across
the park to Karl Marx House.

Coming toward him from a distance on the broad
park path were about twenty nursery-school kids and
their teacher. She had in her hand the end of a long red
string, which the children held on to as they followed
her single file. They walked along slowly, and the

teacher pointed at the various trees and shrubs while giving their names. Jakub stopped to listen because he did not know much botany and always forgot that a maple was called a maple and a hornbeam a hornbeam.

The teacher pointed at a tree thick with yellowing leaves: "This is a linden."

Jakub looked at the children. They all wore little blue coats and red berets. You could take them for little brothers and sisters. He looked at their faces and found that they resembled one another not only because of their clothes but also because of their features. He counted seven among them with markedly big noses and wide mouths. They looked like Dr. Skreta.

He remembered the big-nosed toddler at the forest inn. Could the doctor's eugenic dream be more than just a fantasy? Could it really be that children were coming into the world in this country from the great begetter Skreta?

Jakub found this ridiculous. All these kids looked alike because all children in the world look alike.

And yet he couldn't help but think: What if Skreta really was carrying out his remarkable project? Why can't bizarre projects be carried out?

"And what's this one, children?"

"It's a birch!" answered a little Skreta; yes, he was the picture of Skreta; he not only had the big nose and wide mouth but also wore little eyeglasses and spoke with the nasal voice that made Dr. Skreta's speech so touchingly comical.

"Very good, Oldrich!" said the teacher.

Jakub thought: In ten or twenty years this country will have thousands of Skretas. And once more he had the strange feeling of having lived in his own country without knowing what was happening in it. He had lived, so to speak, at the center of the action. He had lived through all the current events. He had got involved in politics, and it had nearly cost him his life, and even when he was pushed out, politics remained his main concern. He always believed he was hearing the heartbeat of the country. But who knows what he was really hearing? Was it a heart? Or was it an old alarm clock? An old discarded alarm clock that gives the wrong time? Had all his political struggles been anything more than will-o'-the wisps distracting him from what really mattered?

The teacher led the children down the broad path, and Jakub still felt pervaded by the image of the beautiful woman. The recollection of her beauty incessantly brought a question back to mind: What if he had been living in a world entirely different from what he imagined? What if he had been seeing everything upside down? What if beauty meant more than truth, and what if it really had been an angel, the other day, who gave Bertlef a dahlia?

He heard the teacher's voice: "And what's this one?"

The little Skreta in eyeglasses answered: "It's a maple!"

14

Ruzena rushed up the stairs two at a time, trying not to look back. She slammed the door to her section and hurried to the changing room. She slipped her white nurse's smock over her bare body and gave a sigh of relief. The scene with Frantisek had disturbed her, but at the same time, oddly, it had calmed her. She felt that both Frantisek and Klima were now alien and distant.

She left the cubicle and went into the huge treatment room, where women rested after their baths in beds lined up against the walls.

The fortyish nurse was sitting at the small table near the door. "Well, did they authorize it?" she asked her coldly.

"Yes. Thanks for taking my place," said Ruzena, handing a new patient a key and a large white sheet.

As soon as the fortyish nurse left, the door opened and Frantisek's head appeared.

"It's not true that it's none of my business. It's both of our business. I've got something to say about it too!"

"Will you please shove off!" she answered. "This is the women's section, men aren't supposed to be here! Get going this minute or I'll have you thrown out!"

Frantisek's face flushed, and Ruzena's threat made him so furious that he advanced into the room and slammed the door behind him. "I don't care if you have me thrown out! I don't care!" he shouted.

"I'm telling you to get going this minute!" said Ruzena.

"I can see right through both of you! It's that trumpeter character! It's all lies and pulling strings! He arranged everything for you with the doctor; yesterday they gave a concert together! I see it all clearly, and I'm going to stop you from killing my child! I'm the father, and I've got something to say about it! I forbid you to kill my child!"

Frantisek was yelling, and the women lying on the beds under their blankets lifted their heads with curiosity.

By this time Ruzena, too, was completely unnerved because Frantisek was yelling and she didn't know how to calm things down.

"It's not your child," she said. "You've made that up. The child isn't yours."

"What?" yelled Frantisek and, advancing farther into the room, went around the table to come nearer to Ruzena: "What do you mean, not my child! I'm in a pretty good position to know it is! And I know it is!"

Just then a woman, naked and wet, came in from the pool toward Ruzena to be wrapped in a sheet and led to a bed. The woman was startled when she saw Frantisek staring at her unseeingly a few yards away.

For Ruzena it was a moment of respite; she went over to the woman, wrapped her in a sheet, and led her to a bed.

"What's that fellow doing here?" the woman asked, looking back at Frantisek.

"He's a madman! He's gone out of his mind and I don't know how to get him out of here. I don't know what to do with him!" said Ruzena, covering the woman with a warm blanket.

A woman in another bed shouted at Frantisek: "Hey, there! You're not supposed to be here! Get out!"

"I'm supposed to be here, all right!" Frantisek retorted stubbornly and refused to budge. When Ruzena returned he was no longer flushed but pallid; he no longer shouted but spoke softly and resolutely: "I'm only going to tell you one thing. If you get rid of the child, I won't be around anymore either. If you kill this child, you'll have two deaths on your conscience."

Ruzena sighed deeply and looked down at the table. There was her handbag with the tube of pale-blue tablets in it. She shook one into the hollow of her hand and swallowed it.

And Frantisek said, no longer shouting but pleading: "I beg you, Ruzena. I beg you. I can't live without you. I'll kill myself."

Just then Ruzena felt a violent pain in her entrails, and Frantisek saw her face become unrecognizable, contorted by pain, her eyes widening but unseeing, her body twisted, doubled over, her hands pressed against her belly. Then he saw her slump to the floor.

15

Olga was splashing around in the pool when she suddenly heard . . . What exactly did she hear? She didn't know what she was hearing. The room was filled with confusion. The women around her were leaving the pool and looking toward the adjoining treatment room, which seemed to be sucking in everything near it. Olga, too, found herself caught in the flow of this irresistible suction, and unthinkingly, filled with anxious curiosity, she followed the others.

In the adjoining room, she saw a cluster of women at the door with the small table near it. She saw them from behind: they were naked and wet, and bending over with their rumps sticking up. Facing them stood a young man.

More naked women came in jostling one another to join the group, and Olga too worked her way through the crowd and saw Nurse Ruzena lying motionless on the floor. The young man got down on his knees and began to yell: "I killed her! I killed her! I'm a murderer!"

The women were dripping wet. One woman bent over Ruzena's recumbent body to take her pulse. But it was a useless gesture, because death was there and no one doubted it. The naked, wet women's bodies jostled one another impatiently to see death up close, to see it on a familiar face.

Frantisek was still kneeling. He clasped her in his arms and kissed her face.

The women were standing all around him, and he lifted his eyes to them and repeated: "I killed her! I did it! Arrest me!"

"We have to do something!" said one woman, and another ran out into the corridor and started shouting. In a moment two colleagues of Ruzena's came running, followed by a physician in a white smock.

Only then did Olga realize that she was naked and that she was jostling and being jostled by other naked women in front of a young man and a man physician, and the situation suddenly appeared ridiculous to her. But she knew that this would not prevent her from staying here with the crowd and looking at death, which fascinated her.

The physician was holding the recumbent Ruzena's wrist, trying in vain to feel her pulse, and Frantisek kept repeating: "I killed her! Call the police, arrest me!"

16

Jakub found his friend in his office at Karl Marx House just as he was returning from the clinic. He congratulated him on his performance on the drums the day before, and he excused himself for not having come to see him after the concert.

"It really frustrated me," said the doctor. "It's your

last day here, and God knows where you'll be hanging out this evening. We had a lot of things to discuss. And what's worse is that most likely you were with that skinny little thing. Gratitude is a dangerous feeling."

"What gratitude? Why should I be grateful to her?"

"You wrote me that her father had done a lot for you."

That day Dr. Skreta had no office hours, and the gynecological examination table stood unoccupied in the back of the room. The two friends sat down in facing armchairs.

"No," said Jakub. "I only wanted you to take care of her, and it seemed simplest to tell you that I owed a debt of gratitude to her father. But in fact it wasn't that at all. Now that I'm bringing everything to an end, I can tell you about it. I was arrested with her father's total approval. Her father was sending me to my death. Six months later he ended up on the gallows, while I was lucky and escaped it."

"In other words, she's the daughter of a bastard," said the doctor.

Jakub shrugged: "He believed I was an enemy of the revolution. Everybody was saying that, and he let himself be convinced."

"Then why did you tell me he was your friend?"

"We were friends. And nothing was more important to him than to vote for my arrest. This proved that he placed ideals above friendship. When he denounced me as a traitor to the revolution, he felt that he was suppressing his personal interests for the sake of something more sublime, and he experienced it as the great act of his life."

"And is that the reason you like that ugly girl?"

"She had nothing to do with it. She's innocent."

"There are thousands of girls as innocent as she is. If you chose this one, it's probably because she's her father's daughter."

Jakub shrugged, and Dr. Skreta went on: "You're as perverted as he was. I believe that you consider your friendship with this girl the greatest act of your life. You suppressed your natural hatred, your natural loathing, to prove to yourself that you're magnanimous. It's beautiful, but at the same time it's unnatural and entirely pointless."

"You're wrong," Jakub protested. "I wasn't suppressing anything in me, and I wasn't trying to look magnanimous. I was simply sorry for her. From the first time I saw her. She was still a child when they forced her out of her home and she went to live with her mother in some mountain village where the people were afraid to talk to them. For a long time she was unable to get authorization to study, even though she's a gifted girl. It's vile to persecute children because of their parents. Would you want me, too, to hate her because of her father? I was sorry for her. I was sorry for her because her father had been executed, and I was sorry for her because her father had sent a friend to his death."

Just then the telephone rang. Skreta picked up the receiver and listened for a moment. His face darkened, and he said: "I'm busy here right now. Do you really need me?" After a pause he said: "All right. Okay. I'm coming." He hung up and cursed.

"If you've got to go, don't bother about me, I have to leave anyway," said Jakub, rising from his chair.

"No, you're not leaving! We haven't discussed anything yet. And there's something we have to discuss today, right? They made me lose the thread. It was about something important. I've been thinking about it since I woke up. Do you remember what it might be about?"

"No," said Jakub.

"Good God, and now I have to run to the thermal building . . ."

"It's better to say goodbye like this. In the midst of a conversation," said Jakub, and he pressed his friend's hand.

17

Ruzena's lifeless body was lying in a small room reserved for physicians on night duty. Several people were bustling around the room, and a police inspector was there and had already interrogated Frantisek and written down his statement. Frantisek once more expressed his desire to be arrested.

"Did you give her the tablet, yes or no?" asked the inspector.

"No!"

"Then stop saying you killed her."

"She always told me she was going to kill herself," said Frantisek.

"Did she tell you why she was going to kill herself?"

"She said she was going to kill herself if I kept spoiling her life. She said she didn't want a child She'd rather kill herself than have a child!"

Dr. Skreta entered the room. He gave the inspector a friendly wave and went over to the deceased; he lifted her eyelid to examine the color of the conjunctiva.

"Doctor, were you this nurse's supervisor?" asked the inspector.

"Yes."

"Do you think she might have used a poison available in your practice?"

Skreta turned once more to Ruzena's body to examine the particulars of her death. Then he said: "It doesn't look to me like a drug or substance she could have gotten in our offices. It was probably an alkaloid. The autopsy will tell us which one."

"But where did she get it?"

"It's hard to say."

"At the moment, it's all very mysterious," said the inspector. "The motive too. This young man has just revealed that she was expecting a child by him and she wanted to have an abortion."

"That character was forcing her to do it," Frantisek shouted.

"What character?" asked the inspector.

"The trumpeter. He wanted to take her away from me and make her get rid of my child! I followed them! He was with her at the Abortion Committee."

"I can confirm that," said Dr. Skreta. "It's true that this morning we took up her request for an abortion."

"And the trumpeter was with her?" asked the inspector.

"Yes," said Skreta. "Ruzena declared that he was the child's father."

"It's a lie! The child's mine!" Frantisek shouted.

"Nobody doubts that," said Dr. Skreta, "but Ruzena had to declare a married man as the father so the committee would authorize termination of the pregnancy."

"So you knew it was a lie!" Frantisek shouted at Dr. Skreta.

"According to the law, we have to take the woman's word. Once Ruzena told us she was pregnant by Mister Klima and he confirmed her declaration, none of us had the right to assert the contrary."

"But you didn't believe Mister Klima was the father?" asked the inspector.

"No."

"And on what do you base your opinion?"

"Mister Klima has been to this town only twice before, and briefly both times. It's highly unlikely that a sexual relationship could have taken place between him and our nurse. This is too small a town for me not to hear about such a thing. Mister Klima's paternity most likely was just a deception with which Ruzena persuaded him to appeal to the committee to authorize the abortion. This young gentleman here surely would not have consented to an abortion."

But Frantisek was no longer hearing what Skreta was saying. And he stood there unseeing. All he heard were Ruzena's words: "You're going to drive me to suicide, you're definitely going to drive me to suicide," and he knew that he had caused her death and yet he did not understand why, and it all seemed inexplicable to him. He stood there face to face with the unreal, like a savage confronted by a miracle, and all of a sudden he had become deaf and blind because his mind was unable to conceive of the incomprehensibility that had swooped down on him.

(My poor Frantisek, you will wander through your whole life without understanding, you will only know that your love killed the woman you loved, you will carry this certainty like a secret mark of horror; you will wander like a leper bringing inexplicable disasters to loved ones, you will wander through your whole life like a mailman of misfortune.)

He was pale, standing immobile like a pillar of salt and not even seeing that an agitated man had entered the room; the new arrival approached the dead woman, looked at her for a long while, and caressed her hair.

Dr. Skreta whispered: "Suicide. Poison."

The man shook his head violently: "Suicide? I can swear by all I hold dearest that this woman did not take her own life. And if she swallowed poison it has to be murder."

The inspector looked at the man in amazement. It was Bertlef, and his eyes were burning with angry fire.

18

Jakub turned the ignition key and drove off. He passed the spa town's last villas and found himself in a landscape. He headed for the border, and he had no urge to hurry. The thought that he was driving this way for the last time made this landscape dear to him and strange. He kept feeling that he did not recognize it, that it was different from what he had thought, and that it was a pity he could not stay longer.

But he also told himself that no postponement of his departure, whether for a day or several years, could in any way change what it was now making him suffer; he would never know this landscape more intimately than he knew it today. He must accept the thought that he was going to leave it without knowing it, without having exhausted its charms, that he was going to leave it as a debtor and creditor both.

Then he thought again about the young woman to whom he had given the sham poison by slipping it into a medicine tube, and he told himself that his career as a murderer had been the briefest of all his careers. I was a murderer for about eighteen hours, he told himself, and he smiled.

But then he raised an objection: It was not true, he had not been a murderer for only such a brief time. He was a murderer right now and would remain one for the rest of his life. For it mattered little whether the pale-blue tablet was poison or not, what counted was that he believed it was and yet had given it to a stranger and done nothing to save her.

And he set about reflecting on all of it with the unconcern of a man who regards his act as existing merely in the realm of the purely experimental: His act of murder was strange. It was a murder without a motive. It had no aim of gaining something or other for the murderer's benefit. What exactly, then, was its meaning? Obviously, the only meaning of his act of murder was to teach him that he was a murderer.

Murder as an experiment, as an act of self-knowledge, reminded him of something: yes, of Raskolnikov. Raskolnikov, who murdered in order to know whether a man has the right to kill an inferior human being, and whether he would have the strength to bear that murder; by that murder, he was interrogating himself about himself.

Yes, there was something that brought him close to Raskolnikov: the pointlessness of the murder, its theoretical nature. But there were differences: Raskolnikov wondered whether a superior man has the right to sacrifice the life of an inferior one for his own benefit.

When Jakub gave the nurse the tube containing the poison, he had nothing like that in mind. Jakub was not wondering whether a man had the right to sacrifice the life of another. On the contrary, Jakub had always been convinced that no one had that right. Jakub was living in a world where people sacrificed the lives of others for the sake of abstract ideas. Jakub knew the faces of these people, faces now brazenly innocent, now sadly craven, faces that apologetically but meticulously carried out cruel verdicts on their neighbors. Jakub knew these faces, and he detested them. Moreover, Jakub knew that every human being wishes for someone's death, and that only two things deter him from murder: fear of punishment and the physical difficulty of inflicting death. Jakub knew that if everyone had the power to kill in secret and at a distance, mankind would vanish in a few minutes. He therefore concluded that Raskolnikov's experiment was totally useless.

Why then had he given the poison to the nurse? Was it simply by chance? Raskolnikov had actually spent a long time plotting and preparing for his crime, while Jakub had acted on the impulse of a moment. But Jakub realized that he, too, had unknowingly for many years been preparing for his act of murder, and that the instant he gave the poison to Ruzena was a fissure into which had been shoveled all of his past life, all of his disgust with mankind.

When Raskolnikov murdered the old woman usurer with an ax, he knew that he was crossing a horrifying threshold; that he was transgressing divine law; he knew that although the old woman was contemptible, she was a creature of God. The fear that Raskolnikov felt, Jakub had not experienced. For him human beings were not creatures of God. Jakub loved scrupulousness and high-mindedness, and he was persuaded that these were not human qualities. Jakub knew human beings well, and that is why he did not love them. Jakub was high minded, and that is why he gave them poison.

So I am a murderer out of high-mindedness, he said to himself, and the thought seemed ridiculous and sad.

After Raskolnikov killed the old usurer he did not have the strength to control the tremendous storm of remorse. Whereas Jakub, who was deeply convinced that no one had the right to sacrifice the lives of others, felt no remorse at all.

He tried to imagine that the nurse had really died, to see if he felt any guilt. No, he felt nothing of the kind. His mind calm and at peace, he drove on through the pleasant region that was bidding him farewell.

Raskolnikov experienced his crime as a tragedy, and eventually he was overwhelmed by the weight of his act. Jakub was amazed that his act was so light, so weightless, amazed that it did not overwhelm him. And he wondered if this lightness was not more terrifying than the Russian character's hysterical feelings.

He drove slowly, now and then interrupting his reflections to look at the landscape. He told himself that the episode of the tablet had been merely a game, an inconsequential game like his whole life in this land on whose soil he had left not a single trace, not a root or a furrow, a land he was now going away from as a breeze goes away.

19

Lighter by a quarter liter of blood, Klima impatiently waited for Dr. Skreta in his waiting room. He did not wish to leave the spa without saying goodbye and asking him to look after Ruzena a bit. "Until they take it away from me, I can still change my mind." He could still hear these words of hers, and they frightened him. He was afraid that after he left and Ruzena was no longer under his influence, she might at the last minute go back on her decision.

Dr. Skreta finally appeared. Klima rushed toward him, said goodbye, and thanked him for his beautiful work on the drums.

"It was a great concert," said Dr. Skreta, "you played wonderfully. Let's hope we can do it again! We have to think about arranging concerts like that at other spas."

"Yes, I'd be glad to do it, I enjoyed playing with you!" the trumpeter said eagerly, and he added: "I want to ask you a favor. If you could look after Ruzena a bit. I'm afraid she'll get all worked up again. Women are so unpredictable."

"She won't get worked up anymore, don't worry," said Dr. Skreta. "She's no longer alive."

For a moment Klima did not understand, and Dr. Skreta explained what had happened. Then he said: "It's suicide, but there's something rather puzzling about it. Some people might find it odd that she did away with herself an hour after appearing before the committee with you. No, no, no, don't worry," he added, seizing the trumpeter by the hand when he saw him turning pale. "Fortunately for us, Ruzena had a boyfriend, a young repairman who's convinced the child is his. I've stated that there was never anything between you and the nurse, that she simply persuaded you into playing the child's father because the committee doesn't authorize abortions when both parents are single. So don't spill the beans if you're ever interrogated. You're clearly on edge, and that's a pity. You've got to pull yourself together, because we've still got a lot of concerts ahead of us."

Klima was speechless. He kept bowing to Dr. Skreta and kept shaking his hand.

Kamila was waiting for him in the room at the Richmond. Klima took her in his arms and without a word kissed her on the cheek. He kissed her all over her face, then he kneeled and kissed her dress down to her knees.

"What's come over you?"

"Nothing. I'm so lucky to have you. I'm so lucky you exist."

They packed their bags and carried them to their white sedan. Klima said he was tired and asked her to take the wheel.

They drove in silence. Klima was exhausted, yet greatly relieved. He was still somewhat uneasy about the thought that he might yet be interrogated. If that should occur, Kamila might get wind of something. But he repeated to himself what Dr. Skreta had told him. If he were to be interrogated, he would play the innocent (and in this country common enough) role of the gentleman who plays the father to do a good turn. No one could hold it against him, not even Kamila if she happened to hear about it.

He looked at her. Her beauty filled the space of the car like a heady perfume. He told himself that he wished to breathe only that perfume for the rest of his life. Then he heard in his mind the sweet, distant music of his trumpet, and he resolved for the rest of his life to play this music solely to please her, his only and dearest woman.

20

Whenever she took the wheel, she felt stronger and more independent. But this time it was not only the wheel that gave her self-confidence. It was also the words of the stranger she had met in the corridor of the Richmond. She was unable to forget them. Nor was she able to forget his face, so much more virile than the smooth face of her husband. Kamila reflected that never before had she known a man, a real man.

She looked sidelong at the trumpeter's tired face, which kept breaking into inscrutably blissful smiles while his hand lovingly caressed her shoulder.

This excessive tenderness neither pleased nor touched her. Insofar as it was inexplicable, it confirmed yet again that the trumpeter had his secrets, a life of his own that he hid from her and excluded her from. But now, instead of hurting her, the observation left her indifferent.

What had the man said? That he was leaving forever. A sweet, prolonged yearning wrung her heart. Not only a yearning for the man but also for the lost opportunity. And not only for that opportunity but also for opportunity as such. She had a yearning for all the opportunities she had let pass, escaped, evaded, even for those she had never had.

The man had told her that he had lived all his life like a blind man, that he had not even suspected that beauty exists. She understood him. Because it was the same with her. She, too, lived in blindness. She had been seeing only a single being lit up by the floodlight of her jealousy. And what would happen if that floodlight abruptly went out? In the unfocused light of day other beings would suddenly appear by the thousands, and the man she had up until now believed was the only one in the world would become one among many.

She was at the wheel feeling sure of herself and beautiful, and she went on thinking: Was it really love that bound her to Klima or only the fear of losing him? And if it could be said that at the beginning this fear had been the anxious form of love, as time passed had not love (tired, worn-out) slipped away from that form? Was what finally remained only fear, fear without love? And what would remain if she lost that fear?

Beside her the trumpeter smiled inscrutably.

She glanced at him and told herself that if she ceased being jealous nothing at all would remain. She was driving at great speed, and she reflected that somewhere ahead on the road of her life a line indicating the breakup with the trumpeter had already been traced. For the first time, this idea inspired neither anxiety nor fear in her.

21

It was evening. Olga entered Bertlef's suite and excused herself: "Pardon me for barging in on you. But I'm in such a state I can't be alone. I'm not disturbing you, am I?"

In the room were Bertlef, Dr. Skreta, and the inspector; it was the latter who answered Olga: "You're not disturbing us. Our conversation now is unofficial."

"The inspector is an old friend of mine," the doctor explained to Olga.

"Why did she do it?" Olga asked.

"She had a fight with her boyfriend, and in the middle of the argument she took something out of her bag and swallowed poison. That's all we know, and I'm afraid that's all we'll ever know," said the inspector.

"Inspector, please," Bertlef said forcefully, "I beg you to pay attention to what I said in my statement. Here, in this very room, I spent with Ruzena the last night of her life. Perhaps I have not sufficiently emphasized the main thing. It was a wonderful night, and Ruzena was immensely happy. That unassuming girl only needed to throw off the shackles she had been locked into by her indifferent and dreary companions to become a radiant being filled with love, sensitivity, and high-mindedness, to become the person you would not have suspected was inside her. I am positive that last night I opened for her the door to another life, and it was just last night that she began to have a desire for life. But then someone stood in the way . . ." said Bertlef, suddenly pensive, and then he added softly: "I sense in it hell's intervention."

"The police don't have much influence over the infernal powers," the inspector said.

Bertlef did not respond to the irony. "The suicide theory really makes no sense," he replied. "Please understand, I beg you! It is impossible that she would kill herself at the very moment when she was wishing to begin to live! I repeat, I will not allow her to be accused of suicide."

"My dear sir," said the inspector, "no one is accusing her of suicide, for the good reason that suicide is not a crime. Suicide is not something that concerns justice. It's not our concern."

"Yes," said Bertlef, "suicide is not a crime for you because life has no value for you. But I, Inspector, do not know of a greater sin. Suicide is worse than murder. One can murder for vengeance or out of greed, but even greed is the expression of a perverted love of life. But to commit suicide is to throw one's life down contemptuously at God's feet. To commit suicide is to spit in the Creator's face. I tell you that I will do everything I can to prove that this young woman is innocent. Since you maintain that she did away with herself, please explain why. What motive have you found?"

"Motives for suicide are always mysterious," said the inspector. "Besides, looking for them isn't within my purview. Don't hold it against me for confining myself to my duties. I've got enough of those and hardly any time. The case is obviously not yet closed, but I can tell you in advance that I'm not thinking of the homicide theory."

"I admire your quickness," said Bertlef acidly, "your quickness to cross out a human being's life."

Olga saw the inspector's cheeks redden. But he controlled himself, and after a brief pause said in a voice that was almost too amiable: "All right, I accept your theory that a murder has been committed. Let's ask ourselves how it could have been perpetrated. We found a tube of tranquilizers in the victim's handbag. One could assume that the nurse wanted to take a tablet to calm herself but that someone had previously slipped another tablet into the medicine tube, one that looked like the others but contained poison."

"You think that Ruzena got the poison from the tube of tranquilizers?" asked Dr. Skreta.

"Of course, Ruzena could have got the poison not from the tube but from elsewhere in the handbag. That's what would have happened if it was suicide. But if we adopt the murder theory, we have to accept that someone slipped into the medicine tube a poison that could be mistaken for one of Ruzena's tablets. That's the only possibility."

"Pardon me for contradicting you," said Dr. Skreta, "but it's not so easy to turn an alkaloid into a normal-looking tablet. For that, you need access to pharmaceutical machinery, which isn't available to anybody around here."

"Are you saying it's impossible for an ordinary person to get such a tablet?" the inspector asked.

"It's not impossible, but it's extremely difficult."

"It's enough for me to know that it's possible," said the inspector, and he went on: "Now let's ask ourselves who might have had an interest in killing this woman. She wasn't rich, so we can rule out any financial motive. We can also eliminate political motives or espionage. So we're left with motives of a personal nature. Who are the suspects? First of all, Ruzena's lover, who had a violent quarrel with her just before her death. Do you believe he was the one who gave her the poison?"

No one answered the inspector's question, and he continued: "I don't think so. The boy was still fighting to keep Ruzena. He wanted to marry her. She was pregnant by him, and even if the child was another man's, what matters is that the boy was convinced she was pregnant by him. When he learned that she wanted an abortion he felt desperate. But please bear in mind that Ruzena had come back from the Abortion Committee, not from the abortion! For our desperate boy, all was not yet lost. The fetus was still alive and he was ready to do anything to save it. It's absurd to think that he would have given her poison at that point, when all he was hoping for was to live with her and have a child with her. Besides, the doctor has explained to us that it isn't possible for just anybody to procure poison that looks like an ordinary tablet. Where could this naïve boy with no connections procure it? Would you explain that to me?"

Bertlef, whom the inspector kept addressing, shrugged his shoulders.

"Let's go on to other suspects. There's that trumpeter from the capital. It was here that he became acquainted with the deceased, and we'll never know to what point their relations went. In any case they were close enough for the deceased to ask him to pass himself off as the father of the fetus and to appear with her before the Abortion Committee. Why did she ask him rather than someone from around here? It's not hard to guess. Any married man living in this little spa town would be afraid of trouble with his wife if word got around. Only someone from somewhere else could have done Ruzena that favor. What's more, the rumor that she was expecting the child of a famous artist could only be flattering to the nurse and could not harm the trumpeter. We can therefore assume that Mister Klima heedlessly agreed to do her the favor. Is that a reason to murder the poor nurse? It's highly improbable, as the doctor has explained to us, that Klima was really the child's father. But examine even that possibility. Let's assume that Klima was the father and that this was extremely disagreeable to him. Can you explain to me why he would kill the nurse when she had agreed to terminate the pregnancy and the operation had already been authorized? Now, Mister Bertlef, do you really want to say that Klima is the murderer?"

"You're misunderstanding me," said Bertlef calmly. "I do not wish to send anyone to the electric chair. I only wish to exonerate Ruzena. Because suicide is the greatest sin. Even a life of suffering has a mysterious value. Even a life on the threshold of death is a thing of splendor. Anyone who has not looked death in the face does not know this, but I know it, Inspector, and that is why I tell you I will do everything I can to prove that this young woman is innocent."

"I'm trying to do that too," said the inspector. "And actually there's still a third suspect. Mister Bertlef, an American businessman. He's admitted that the deceased spent the last night of her life with him. One might object that this is something the murderer probably wouldn't voluntarily admit to us. But that objection doesn't pass scrutiny. Everyone at the concert yesterday evening saw Mister Bertlef sitting next to Ruzena and leaving with her. Mister Bertlef knows very well that under such circumstances it's better to admit something promptly rather than to be unmasked by others. Mister Bertlef claims that Nurse Ruzena had a very satisfying night. That shouldn't surprise us! Mister Bertlef is not only a fascinating man but above all he's an American businessman who has dollars and a passport with which you can travel all over the world. Ruzena is walled up in this place, looking in vain for a way out. She has a boyfriend who wants only to marry her, but he's just a young local repairman. If she marries him her fate would be sealed forever, she will never get out. She has nobody else, so she doesn't break up with him. But she avoids binding herself to him permanently because she doesn't want to give up her hopes. And then suddenly an exotic man with refined manners appears, and he turns her head. She believes that he'll marry her and that she'll permanently leave behind this forsaken corner of the world. At first she knows how to behave like a discreet mistress, but then she becomes more and more of a nuisance. She makes it clear that she will not give him up, and she starts to blackmail him. But Bertlef is married and, if I'm not mistaken, he loves his wife, who is the mother of his one-year-old boy and is expected to arrive here from America tomorrow. Bertlef wants at all costs to avoid a scandal. He knows that Ruzena always carries a tube of tranquilizers, and he knows what the tablets look like. He has a lot of connections abroad, and he has a lot of money. For him it's no problem to have a poison tablet made that looks the same as Ruzena's medicine. In the course of that wonderful night, while his mistress was sleeping, he slipped the poison into the tube. I think, Mister Bertlef," the inspector concluded with a solemnly raised voice, "that you are the only person with a motive to murder the nurse and also the only person with the means. I ask you to confess."

Silence pervaded the room. The inspector looked Bertlef in the eye for a long while, and Bertlef returned the look with equal patience and silence. His face expressed neither amazement nor irritation. At last he said: "I am not surprised by your conclusion. Since you are incapable of finding the murderer, you have to find someone to assume reponsibility for the offense. It is one of the mysterious laws of life that the innocent must pay for the guilty. Please do arrest me."

22

The countryside was suffused with soft twilight. Jakub halted in a village only a few kilometers from the border crossing. He wished to prolong the last moments he would be spending in his country. He got out of the car to take a little stroll down the village street.

It was not a pretty street. Lying around in front of the low-roofed houses were rolls of rusted wire, an old tractor wheel, pieces of scrap metal. It was a neglected, ugly village. Jakub told himself that the scattering of rusted wire was like a coarse word his native land was addressing to him by way of farewell. He walked to the end of the street to a small pond. The pond, neglected too, was covered with green scum. Some geese were splashing around at its edge, and a boy with a switch was trying to herd them away.

Jakub turned around to go back to his car. Just then he became aware of a little boy standing behind a window. Barely five years old, he was looking out the window toward the pond. Perhaps he was watching the geese, perhaps he was watching the boy flailing at the geese with his switch. He was behind the window, and Jakub could not take his eyes off him. What fascinated Jakub about the child's face were the eyeglasses. They were large eyeglasses, probably with thick lenses. The child's head was little and the eyeglasses were big. He was wearing them like a burden. He was wearing them like a fate. He was looking through the frames of his eyeglasses as if through a wire fence. Yes, he was wearing the frames as if they were a wire fence he would have to drag along with him all his life. And Jakub looked through the wire fence of the eyeglasses at the little boy's eyes, and he was suddenly filled with great sadness.

It was as sudden as the spread of water over countryside when riverbanks give way. It had been a long time since Jakub had been sad. Many years. He had known only sourness, bitterness, but not sadness. And now it had assailed him, and he could not move.

He saw in front of him the child dressed in his wire fence, and he pitied that child and his whole country, reflecting that he had loved this country little and badly, and he was sad because of that bad and failed love.

And all at once the thought came to him that it was pride that had kept him from loving this country, pride in nobility, pride in high-mindedness, pride in scrupulousness; an insane pride that made him dislike his kind and detest them because he saw them as murderers. And once again he remembered that he had slipped poison into a stranger's medicine tube, and that he himself was a murderer. He was a murderer, and his pride was reduced to dust. He had become one of them. He was a brother of those distressing murderers.

The little boy with the big eyeglasses stood at the window as if petrified, his eyes still fixed on the pond. And Jakub realized that this child had done no harm, that he was not guilty of anything, and yet he had been born with bad eyes and would have them forever. And he reflected further that what he had held against others was something given, something they came into the world with and carried with them like a heavy wire fence. He reflected that he had no privileged right to high-mindedness and that the highest degree of high-mindedness is to love people even though they are murderers.

He thought once again of the pale-blue tablet, and

he told himself that he had slipped it into the disagreeable nurse's medicine tube as an apology; as an application to be admitted into their ranks; as a plea to be
accepted by them even though he had always refused
to be counted as one of them.

He quickly headed back to the car, opened the door,
took the wheel, and set out again for the border. The
day before he had thought that this would be a moment
of relief. That he would be glad to be going away. That
he would be leaving a place where he had been born by
mistake, and where, in fact, he did not feel at home.
But now he knew that he was leaving his only homeland and that he had no other.

23

"Don't be thrilled," said the inspector. "The glorious
prison gates won't be opening for you to go through
like Jesus Christ climbing Calvary. It never occurred
to me that you could kill that young woman. I only
accused you so you'd stop insisting so stubbornly that
she was murdered."

"I am glad you were not serious about the accusation," said Bertlef in a conciliatory tone. "And you are
right, it was not reasonable for me to try to obtain justice for Ruzena through you."

"I'm pleased to see you settle your differences," said Dr. Skreta. "There's one thing at least we can take comfort from. However Ruzena died, her last night was a beautiful night."

"Look at the moon," said Bertlef. "It is just as it was yesterday, and it is turning this room into a garden. Barely twenty-four hours ago Ruzena was the fairy queen of this garden."

"And we shouldn't be so interested in justice," Dr. Skreta said. "Justice is not a human thing. There's the justice of blind, cruel laws, and maybe there's also another justice, a higher justice, but that one I don't understand. I've always felt that I was living here in this world *beyond justice*."

"What do you mean?" asked Olga, amazed.

"Justice doesn't concern me," said Dr. Skreta. "It's something outside and above me. In any case it's something inhuman. I'll never cooperate with this repellent power."

"Are you trying to say," Olga asked, "that you don't recognize any universal values?"

"The values I recognize have nothing in common with justice."

"For example?" Olga asked.

"For example, friendship," Dr. Skreta replied softly.

Everyone remained silent, and the inspector rose to go. Just then, Olga had a sudden thought: "What color were the tablets Ruzena was taking?"

"Pale blue," said the inspector, and then added with renewed interest: "But why do you ask?"

Olga was afraid that the inspector had read her mind, and quickly backtracked: "I saw her once with a medicine tube. I was wondering if it was the tube I saw . . ."

The inspector had not read her mind, he was tired and bade everyone good evening.

After he had left, Bertlef said to the doctor: "Our wives will be arriving soon. Shall we go to meet them?"

"Certainly. And I want you to take a double dose of your medication tonight," said the doctor with concern as Bertlef went off into the small adjoining room.

"You once gave some poison to Jakub," said Olga. "It was a pale-blue tablet. And he always had it with him. I know it."

"Don't talk nonsense. I never gave him any such thing," the doctor said very forcefully.

Then Bertlef, wearing a fresh necktie, returned from the adjoining room, and Olga took her leave of the two men.

24

Bertlef and Dr. Skreta walked down the poplar-lined avenue to the railroad station.

"Look at that moon," said Bertlef. "Believe me, Doctor, the evening and night yesterday were miraculous."

"I believe you, but you should take it easy. The bodily movements that inevitably go with such a beautiful night can really be very risky for you."

Bertlef did not reply, and his face radiated only happy pride.

"You seem to be in an excellent mood," said Dr. Skreta.

"You're not mistaken. If, thanks to me, the last night of her life was a beautiful night, I'm happy."

"You know," Dr. Skreta said suddenly, "there's a strange thing I want to ask you but have never dared to. And yet I have the sense that today is so exceptional that I might be bold enough to . . ."

"Speak up, Doctor!"

"I want you to adopt me as your son."

Bertlef stopped in bewilderment, and Dr. Skreta explained the reasons for his request.

"I would do anything for you, Doctor!" said Bertlef. "I am only afraid that my wife might find it odd. She would be much younger than her son. Is this even legally possible?"

"It doesn't say anywhere that an adopted son must be younger than his parents. He isn't a son by blood, but just an adopted son."

"Are you sure of that?"

"I consulted lawyers a long time ago," Dr. Skreta said shyly.

"You know, it is a peculiar idea, and I am a little surprised by it," said Bertlef, "but today I am under such a spell that I want nothing but to make everyone happy. So if that makes you happy . . . my son . . ."

And the two men embraced in the middle of the street.

25

Olga lay stretched out on her bed (the radio in the next room was silent), and it was obvious to her that Jakub had killed Ruzena and that only she and Dr. Skreta knew it. She would probably never learn why he had done it. A shudder of horror ran through her, but then she noticed with surprise (as we know, she knew how to observe herself) that the shudder was delightful and the horror full of pride.

The night before, she had made love with Jakub while he must have been full of the most excruciating thoughts, and she had absorbed him completely into herself, even with those thoughts.

Why doesn't this repel me? she wondered. Why don't I go (and never will go) and inform on him? Am I, too, living beyond justice?

But the more she interrogated herself this way, the more she felt swelling in her that strange, happy pride, and she felt like a young girl who is being raped and is abruptly gripped by stunning pleasure growing all the more powerful the more strongly it is being resisted . . .

26

The train reached the railroad station, and two women got off.

One was about thirty-five and received a kiss from Dr. Skreta; the other, who was younger and elegantly dressed, carried a baby in her arms and was kissed by Bertlef.

"Show us your little boy, Mrs. Bertlef," said the doctor, "I haven't seen him yet!"

"If I didn't know you so well, I'd be suspicious," said Suzy Skreta, laughing. "Look, he has a birthmark on his upper lip, in exactly the same place as you!"

Mrs. Bertlef examined Dr. Skreta's face and said in a near shout: "It's true! I never noticed it on you when I was here at the spa before!"

Bertlef said: "It is such an amazing coincidence that I venture to rank it among the miracles. Doctor Skreta, who restores health to women, belongs to the category of angels, and like an angel, he puts his sign on the children he has helped bring into the world. It is not a birthmark, it is an angel mark."

All were delighted by Bertlef's explanation, and they laughed cheerfully.

"Besides," Bertlef went on, addressing his charming wife, "I hereby solemnly announce that, as of a few minutes ago, the doctor is the brother of our little John. Since they are brothers, it is quite normal for them to bear the same mark."

"Finally! You finally decided . . ." said Suzy Skreta to her husband with a sigh of happiness.

"I don't understand, I don't understand any of this!" said Mrs. Bertlef, insisting on an explanation.

"I shall explain everything to you. We have many things to talk about today, many things to celebrate. We have a marvelous weekend before us," said Bertlef, taking his wife by the arm. Then the four of them walked off under the platform lights and away from the railroad station.

COMPLETED IN BOHEMIA IN 1971 OR 1972